"**The queer romance we deserve** . . . Instead of a warning about what could happen if you are gay, this is a celebration of what awaits you if you are."
—*Autostraddle*

"Perri's book is a real gift—**tender, sexy as hell, and laugh out loud funny.**"
—**Cynthia D'Aprix Sweeney, author of** *The Nest*

"**Compelling.**" —*Us Weekly*

"The attraction between Katie and Cassidy unfolds in a believable, and utterly romantic, way. . . . **Love is love, and true love is always worth fighting for.**"
—*Washington Independent Review of Books*

"If you're trying to get over an ex, **read this** instead of compulsively checking your iPhone."
—*Marie Claire*

"This **smart, funny** novel fills a space in the romantic comedy genre by giving readers something missing: a celebration of queerness, in all its dynamic glory." —*Nylon*

"For fans of: **pop culture references, hot lesbian sex scenes, bar fights**." —*Out*

"**Lively and funny.**" —*NPR*

"Get ready to **laugh, cry, and rediscover your faith in romance**." —*Lambda Literary Review*

"A film-ready rom-com." —ELLE

"The lightness and ease of a lesbian romance that does not up-end any trauma is a refreshing, upbeat relief. *When Katie Met Cassidy* resonates—and not just for queers. Its pursue-or-be-pursued tension will have you reading until the happy ever after."
—*Broadly*

"Not only is Perri's book super sexy—it's also a welcome sub-version of the (so far) overwhelmingly straight rom-com genre."
—*Refinery29*

"*When Katie Met Cassidy* is a rom-com. But it's also an im-portant commentary on the taboos of women owning their sexuality."
—*HelloGiggles*

"[A] delightful summer read."
—*Elite Daily*

"This sapphic rom-com is a bubbly and refreshing twist on queer lit."
—*Medium*

"Snarky but tender, charming but never saccharine, *When Katie Met Cassidy* is a romantic comedy for a new breed of women who can deliver valentines *and* a mean left hook."
—Courtney Maum,
author of *Touch* and *I Am Having So Much Fun Here Without You*

"A perfect mixture of humor, romance, and drama—it re-minds us all that love knows no bounds and can be found in even the most unexpected places."
—*Signature Reads*

"This novel tackles the question: Why, when it comes to female sexuality, are so few women figuring out what they want and then going out and doing it?" —*Hypable*

"A fun, fast, sexy read, but it's also so much more—a moving story about love and identity and what it means to truly connect with someone, even if it's the last person you expect."
—Jennifer Niven,
New York Times–bestselling author of *All the Bright Places*

"A gutsy book that breathes a breath of fresh air into the genre of romance novels . . . Brimming with joy and humor, this quick-paced plot opens a window into the LGBTQ community, developing characters who are relatable and grounding it with a core romance that is truly heartwarming."
—*RT Book Reviews*

"Perri's clean writing style and superb wit carry the book beyond the usual [rom-com] and into something laugh-out-loud funny, sincere, and fresh." —*Lambda Literary Review*

"An intensely fun, sexy, and nuanced rom-com." —*The Lily*

"An extremely cute, low-angst lesbian romance. You should read it. Again and again and again." —*LGBTQ Reads*

"A delicious, fast-paced love story about two women who, at first glance, make an unlikely pair but are destined to make sparks fly. Perri's novel is fun, funny, and super charming. I inhaled this romance!" —Jennifer Mathieu, author of *Moxie*

ALSO BY CAMILLE PERRI

The Assistants

WHEN
Katie
MET
Cassidy

➤➤❤→

CAMILLE PERRI

G. P. Putnam's Sons
New York

PUTNAM
— EST. 1838 —

G. P. Putnam's Sons
Publishers Since 1838
An imprint of Penguin Random House LLC
penguinrandomhouse.com

The Library of Congress has catalogued the G. P. Putnam's Sons
hardcover edition as follows:

Names: Perri, Camille, author.
Title: When Katie met Cassidy / Camille Perri.
Description: New York : G.P. Putnam's Sons, [2018]
Identifiers: LCCN 2017045119| ISBN 9780735212817 (hardcover) |
ISBN 9780735212831 (ebook)
Subjects: LCSH: Women—Sexual behavior—Fiction. | Self-realization in
women—Fiction. | Female friendship—Fiction. | BISAC: FICTION /
Contemporary Women. | GSAFD: Humorous fiction. | Love stories.
Classification: LCC PS3616.E768 W48 2018 | DDC 813/.6—dc23
LC record available at https://lccn.loc.gov/2017045119
p.   cm.

First G. P. Putnam's Sons hardcover edition / June 2018
First G. P. Putnam's Sons trade paperback edition / June 2019
G. P. Putnam's Sons trade paperback edition ISBN: 9780735212824

Printed in the United States of America
2nd Printing

Book design by Michelle McMillian

WHEN
Katie
MET
Cassidy

ONE

Katie left the stale pile of her pajamas behind her like a cow pie on the bathroom floor and put herself into the shower. Morning routines would continue, she thought as she washed her hair for the first time in days. Oral hygiene would carry on. Brush, rinse, spit. Once in a while floss. A whitening strip if you're really feeling dazzling. These were the days of our lives, for as long as we lived, until we died. Alone.

Wrapped in a towel, she fished through the maze of cardboard boxes littering the floor of her one-bedroom West Village apartment until she found the one containing her work clothes. She pulled out the black Dior skirt suit that she always wore to closings, which would require a great deal of effort to de-wrinkle.

Now, where was her steamer? With each box she searched through, Katie felt herself becoming more hysterical, until the truth was undeniable: Paul Michael had forgotten to pack it. Or, correction, he had forgotten to direct whomever he'd hired to box up her things to pack it.

Unless he left it out on purpose? He was always borrowing her steamer even though it was carnation pink and only cost twenty dollars and he could have easily bought himself one in black or gray.

"I'm going to buy you your own steamer," she'd once said to him while standing in the doorway to the bathroom with her blouse at her side, waiting for him to finish smoothing out the final creases in his chinos.

"Nah," he said. "No sense in having more than one."

Wearing a suit with shar-pei–sized wrinkles to her meeting was unacceptable, but what was Katie supposed to do? There was a little bit of steam still in the bathroom, so she shuttled everything in there. She hung her jacket, blouse, and skirt from the shower curtain rod and then sat on the edge of the tub with all of it swinging over her like a hanged woman.

Today's closing was with a group of lawyers representing Falcon Capital. Falcon fucking Capital. Hedge funds loved to give themselves names that implemented intimidating animals, names like Lion Management or Tiger Fund. Katie swore if she ever started a fund, she'd go against type with something like Lemur Partners or Sleeping Sloth LLC. Or, in homage to her home state's favorite backyard game, Corn-hole Capital. You'd think someone might appreciate the humor in naming a fund as such, but Katie's experience so far was that finance guys—and most of them were guys—lacked a sense of humor. They were too busy counting their money. And their lawyers were even worse because the law-yers were the ones who had to do all the arguing on their clients' behalf.

In other words, it was safe to assume no one in the board-room today would even crack a smile if Katie explained that she was sorry but her suit was rumpled because her life had imploded over the weekend and her ex-fiancé refused to give up custody of the one item she'd ever bought on HSN that meant shit to her.

When Katie finally arrived at Falcon Capital's office building, she checked her watch to see exactly how late she was, but she'd forgotten her watch, so she only checked her bare wrist. Inside she was met with a vast reception area jam-packed with the most massive crowd of suits and ties anyone had ever seen outside of Grand Central Terminal or the Republican National Convention—all of them waiting for the next elevator.

Katie heard one of the suits say "mechanical malfunc-tion," and she understood this to mean that her day was not about to get any easier. She trudged directly to the recep-tionist desk, where a preppy young man had a phone in the

crook of his shoulder against one ear and a Bluetooth ear-
piece in the other. He held his pointer finger up to her to say,
One moment.

Katie mouthed the words, *I'm looking for the stairs*, but
he paid her no attention. She went so far as to mime walking
up steps, but he still ignored her.

Just then a slickly dressed man in a trim suit bulldozed
up to the desk, knocked on it with his knuckles, and de-
manded, "The stairs. Where are they?"

The receptionist looked right up and pointed to an unas-
suming door on the opposite side of the room.

The guy was off without so much as a thank-you. Katie
jogged after him, benefiting from his complete lack of po-
liteness when it came to forging a path through the crowd
and praying her three-inch Dior heels would not let her wipe
out. She lost sight of him on the stairwell, but when he threw
open the door to Falcon Capital's floor she realized they were
going to the same place.

Katie entered the boardroom just a few steps behind him
to find everyone else already seated—a line of old white men
and young white men, various bald and balding heads of in-
numerable ages. There were handshakes all around.

"Cassidy Price," he of the trim suit and shiny dark hair
said. His handshake was firm, but his skin was soft. Katie
looked straight into his deep-set brown eyes, as one should

do when giving a professional handshake, and only then did it hit her. Cassidy Price was a she.

Katie was thrown and embarrassed, and thankful, too, that she hadn't put her foot in her mouth. It would have been just like her to crack some joke about being the only female in the room and have everyone avert their eyes and pretend they hadn't heard her.

Ms. Price and Katie sat directly across from each other near the center of the conference table, and everyone got down to business.

"What's your first comment to Section 1?" the baldy at the head of the table who was also Katie's boss said, and the meeting proceeded from there like all these meetings did.

"Okay, let's discuss . . ."

"What's next? Section 2(a). Okay, what's your issue there?"

. . . And so on.

Katie was struck by Ms. Price's arrogance, her brashness, the way she reveled in uttering the phrase "Falcon cannot agree to that," as if it were a command.

While she argued the preposterousness of their every position, Katie tried to imagine her life. She looked to be about Katie's age. Was she wearing any makeup? Katie couldn't tell for sure. If not, she had enviable skin. And what sort of product did she use in her hair? Clay? Putty? Pomade? It had such texture and volume—and an expensive cut, no doubt.

She had to be a lesbian. Which, after the weekend Katie had had, seemed so much easier than being straight. For the more comfortable clothes alone. Her black suit fit her perfectly, but it was clearly not a woman's suit. Ditto on the blue button-down dress shirt she wore with it.

"Falcon can absolutely not agree to that," Counselor Price said.

It was no wonder Katie had mistaken her for a man earlier. Mannish was clearly the look she was going for, and her voice was deep and brusque enough that it could go either way.

"Walk us through the issue you have here," Katie's boss said.

The Falcon businessmen and even the other older, more experienced Falcon lawyers let Ms. Price do the walking through for them, because who could stop her?

As she went on, Katie wondered how someone like her had gotten this far looking the way she did—in a field where the dress code was so strict and deeply entrenched that if you wore the wrong shade of stockings you might as well have stayed home. Katie remembered her law school adviser explaining this to her before she went on her first job interview. "You absolutely must wear a skirt suit," her adviser had said. "No pants. It may be the twenty-first century, but Big Law is stuck somewhere around 1955." So how had Cassidy Price managed to jump the divide into the far more simplified dress code for men? She was polished, Katie would give her that, and her suits must have been bespoke—but still. If it were 1955, Ms. Price would have been thrown into the back of a paddy wagon and carted off to jail for this outfit.

"Do you agree with me on this?" Katie's boss asked. He was asking her specifically.

"Yes," Katie said, "I do, absolutely."

Ms. Price echoed her previous sentiments by stating, "Falcon cannot agree to that."

This time, with no idea from where, Katie came back at her with the perfect legalese as to why they would stand firm on this point.

Ms. Price would not stagger. She remained entirely unfazed but said for the first time all morning, "I think Falcon might be able to agree to that."

Then she deferred to her boss, and he said, "Great. Moving on then."

Ha, Katie thought. *Yes.* And was that a slight grin she caught flashing across Counselor Price's face? She had a decent smile. Good clean teeth. A model's bone structure. She would make an attractive woman if she'd grow her hair out and change into a more feminine suit like Katie's. A suit designed for a woman, with breast darts and no pockets and an absurdly low-cut neckline, like God intended it.

꒰♡꒱

The meeting with Falcon Capital broke for the night an hour or two past what a civilian would call dinnertime. They'd have to reconvene the next day, but for now Katie was free. Except that freedom was just another word for walking around in circles when you'd just been dumped by your fiancé.

Katie stared at her phone, alone among the frenetic tide of businessmen rushing every which way from the Falcon building, off to their nighttime nonwork lives. Her first instinct had been to text Paul Michael, but then she remembered there was no more Paul Michael, not in her life anyway. So what now? Should she just go home? Cook something? It had been a long, difficult day—the kind she'd normally have used as an excuse to meet Paul Michael at Le Coucou or Shuko and reward herself with her favorite bottle of French wine or masterfully prepared *omakase*. Or she would call Amy and invite her for a girls' night out at Otto, where they'd share pizza and pasta, followed by the banana coppetta. It shouldn't have felt sad to go to any of those places alone, but it did. Maybe because it was the first night. Or maybe because Paul Michael and Amy were likely at one of those places right now, together, toasting to their new love with Katie's favorite wine or nibbling romantically on each other's *omakase*.

Katie considered her takeout options.

Within the hour she was in her pajamas on her sofa, licking barbecue sauce from her fingers, sipping a pint of cheap bourbon, and flipping the channels looking for some bad TV to watch.

If someone had told her a week ago that she would be sitting here now in this dusty, stale apartment that she hadn't lived in for two years, eating and drinking her pain, surrounded by unpacked cardboard boxes, she wouldn't have believed it. She wouldn't have believed that the man she planned to marry could betray her the way he had, either, or that he could spring it on her the way he did, just before they were supposed to head out to the Hamptons to celebrate Labor Day weekend with Lincoln and Lillian. So maybe she wasn't such a great judge of what was or wasn't believable, possible, or waiting just around the corner to clobber her into oblivion.

Three straight days of binge drinking later, not leaving the apartment until work this morning, and here she was—a living, breathing Before photo for an antidepressant ad.

When would it stop?

Katie put down her chicken wing. This comfort food wasn't bringing her much comfort at all. What would Sheryl Sandberg say if she saw Katie now, or that woman who did the TED Talk about power posing? Surely they'd tell her to get the heck up. They'd say, *Wipe your damn face. Put on the sexiest dress in your closet and the hottest fuck-me pumps you own, and go make some new friends.* Katie hadn't come this far in life to give up now, to sink down beneath a blanket of soiled paper napkins, clutching a remote control that was sticky with barbecue sauce. She was strong! She was a modern woman who knew the power of posing like Wonder Woman before leaving the house each day. She needed to act like it—and for tonight, acting like it meant Katie would have to go out alone.

There was that new wine bar she'd been meaning to check out. It had probably been open for more than a year now, but she still hadn't been there because Paul Michael always said it looked too hip. Or not hip enough. One of those. She couldn't remember which.

Katie scrubbed the barbecue sauce from her face, shook out her hair, slipped on her best low-cut black dress and her highest, sluttiest heels, and out the door she went.

TWO

Even though Cassidy didn't get in till two a.m., she set her alarm for six so she could put in an hour at the gym before making it to the Falcon Capital offices by nine. The late nights and early mornings were becoming more difficult since she'd turned thirty, but she refused to slow down. Instead she worked and played and hit the gym harder than ever, heedful of each—her job, her sex life, and her bodily fitness—with equal energy and attention.

She stepped out of her taxi at West Fifty-Seventh Street on Tuesday morning as pleased by her rowdy Labor Day weekend as she was by her morning's fitness achievements. Now she was ready to work.

Work today would entail the first round of deal making on behalf of her firm's hedge fund client Falcon Capital, a bunch of swinging dicks with shit for brains as far as Cassidy was concerned, but she'd still give them her all. She arrived at the negotiating table uncharacteristically tardy thanks to a broken shuttle elevator, but she was relieved to hear someone arriving just behind her, a woman, no doubt, on account of the accompanying click-clack of high heels, and Cassidy thought, *Yes*, because women were so much easier to intimidate than men—but then she turned to look at her.

The girl was blond-haired-blue-eyed beautiful in a way that made Cassidy feel exposed, like a spotlight had appeared overhead. They shook hands, and for a split second, Cassidy thought she noticed something in the girl's expression change, an element of surprise. Had Cassidy's own expression given her away?

The male lawyers in the room—among them Cassidy's senior partner, a balding, middle-aged man who clearly had not seen the inside of a gym in a while, and her office nemesis, Hamlin Ludsthorp—appeared to suffer no such self-consciousness on account of this Katie Daniels. Because brightening at the sight of a beautiful woman was their birthright. It was what they were supposed to do. Just as it was natural for Ms. Daniels to acknowledge and deflect them without a second thought. Only Cassidy was stuck somewhere in between, somewhere undefined and embarrassing.

Everyone took their seats at the conference table. Of

course Hamlin claimed the chair Cassidy had moved toward first. Hamlin with his damn suspenders and double Windsor knots, like he was some old-world grandfather and not a thirty-two-year-old dickhead from New Jersey.

Cassidy was left with no choice but to sit directly across from Ms. Daniels as they negotiated their deal, section by section.

It wasn't just her looks, Cassidy decided. Lots of girls were beautiful. Plenty had brightened a boardroom before. Sure, her golden hair fell from her bun in perfect wisps in front of her eyes, and her legs stretched as far as Cassidy's eye could see—but in fact, her suit was entirely rumpled and her hair, though sexy and adorable falling onto her face like that, was doubtfully intended to do so. There was an overall unsettledness about her that Cassidy couldn't quite put her finger on, a scattered energy that she seemed to be fighting to contain.

And that accent. It was slight but added an unmistakable sweetness to all her vowels, a preciousness that didn't at all match up to the sleek sophistication she was trying to project.

Cassidy detected that she wasn't wearing a wedding ring, which meant she was single, or as good as single, and she looked young, probably only a year or two out of law school.

"Ms. Price?"

Shit.

"Yes. Yes, I think Falcon can agree to that." Cassidy glanced at her notes, hoping they weren't on the page where she had drawn a big circle and written, *Don't Agree to This!*

When she looked back up, Katie Daniels was smiling, triumphant on winning this point, and there was that brightness again.

-ᄿ-

When they broke for the night, Cassidy waited for Katie Daniels to exit the conference room before she did. Then, briefcase in hand, Cassidy bolted down the stairs in order to already be in the main-floor lobby when Katie emerged from the elevator. Sunglasses at the ready, Cassidy trailed a safe distance behind Katie and followed her out of the building.

Just outside, Katie stopped, so Cassidy stopped. Katie took out her phone, and Cassidy ducked behind a conveniently located modern art sculpture. Cassidy couldn't say for sure why she was semi-stalking her opposing counsel other than that she was intrigued by her. She had the urge to watch Katie while Katie felt unobserved—not in a creepy way, though come to think of it, it was beginning to feel a little creepy.

Katie appeared to be at a loss, like her plans had just gotten canceled. Her shoulders were slumped beneath her sharp, all-business suit jacket, and when she stopped looking at her phone like it was some foreign object that had just appeared in her hand, she simply stared into space.

Cassidy considered ambling over and bumping into Katie by accident, saying *her* plans had just gotten canceled and was there any chance that Katie might want to join her for a bite to eat? But before Cassidy could do something so pathetic and professionally dicey, Katie was off, some decision made, perhaps a new plan secured.

Accepting defeat, Cassidy hailed a cab with one hand and texted Gina with the other: *Out of work. Heading home to change. Dinner before the Met?*

You buyin? Gina immediately wrote back.

Always.

You gonna make me eat sushi again?

Cassidy smiled. *When was the last time you ate something green?*

Dunno, day before yesterday I think. Unless you count the apple Sour Patch Kids I had for lunch.

We're going for sushi.

An hour later Cassidy was sitting across from Gina, watching her pound down a plate of chicken teriyaki and ignore the seaweed salad and broccoli *ohitashi* she'd ordered for her.

Gina was the closest Cassidy had to a best friend. Even though Gina was only twenty-five and had grown up in an environment as different from hers as possible, she'd felt an automatic connection to Gina when they first met at Metropolis two years ago. At the time, Gina had been new to the city, new to the bar, and Cassidy noticed her pilfering half-finished drinks that people left unattended. She was a scrappy-looking thing, knit beanie on her little peanut head, baggy jeans hanging off her ass, sneakers torn to high hell, and Cassidy thought Gina might be homeless. As an experiment Cassidy ordered a gin and tonic, took a sip, then left it on the bar. From a few feet away she watched the kid catch sight of the drink and casually mosey up to it. Right when Gina had the gin and tonic in hand, Cassidy approached.

"Hi," was all Cassidy said, but Gina startled.

"Aww shit, this your drink?" Her accent was thick and Southern. "I think I mistook it for mine."

"No, that's yours," Cassidy said.

Gina hesitated, like she was deciding whether she should bolt.

Cassidy put out her hand. "I'm Cassidy."

"I know who you are," Gina said. "Read all about you on the bathroom wall. You some kind of predator?" Gina looked up at her square in the eyes. "You set a trap to catch me with this drink? You want to fuck me you could just ask, but I'll tell you right now you're not my type."

It was in that moment that Gina won Cassidy over, and they'd been inseparable ever since. It turned out Gina wasn't homeless, but she was a former teenage runaway out of rural Mississippi with fuckheads for parents, so Cassidy did what she could to help the kid out. She kept an eye on her, made sure she ate, had her rent paid, and went to the doctor when she was sick. In return, Gina was loyal. Cassidy trusted her as much as she could trust anyone.

"Sure it's safe for you to hit up the Met tonight after all the drama this weekend?" Gina asked now, without looking up from her teriyaki. "What if you-know-who shows?"

Cassidy shrugged. "I'm not concerned."

"You two need to bury the hatchet already, just go back to being friends."

"There's nothing to bury." Cassidy sipped her green tea.

"Remind me to never get on your bad side," Gina said. "The way you cut people off is goddamn scary."

"Don't ever wrong me and you won't have to worry about it."

"You need therapy, C. I'm not even kidding."

"Eat your broccoli," Cassidy said.

She got a kick out of taking care of Gina. It made her feel useful, and Gina's messed-up home life had struck a nerve. Cassidy knew well the shame and self-reproach that came with having lukewarm parents; many of their friends did. This was something Cassidy had figured out early on as she got to know the others at the Met—so many of them had fled people or places that hadn't embraced them. But by some magic trick they all found their way here, to the city, to the bar, where they discovered one another and—suddenly—felt better about themselves. Beneath all the lesbian drama, that's what Metropolis was really about. Finding your people and making them your family.

After dinner it was still on the early side to hit up the Met, so Cassidy and Gina pregamed at the Up & Up, a cocktail bar on Macdougal that served Cassidy's favorite gin and tonic in the city. By the time they exited two drinks later to the fresh September air, Cassidy was loose and energized, the stress from her day a distant memory. The last person she expected to pass before her eyes was Katie Daniels. She nearly tripped over her own Chelsea boots.

"Whoa. Hold up." Cassidy grabbed Gina by the hood of her sweatshirt.

It was definitely her, Katie Daniels, looking confused and out of sorts just like she had outside the Falcon building earlier that day.

"What's up?" Gina said. "Who'd you see that we're avoiding?"

"I know her." Cassidy nodded toward Katie, who was wearing a sexy black dress and had her blond hair free from its uptight bun.

"The chick that looks like she got lost on the way to auditions for *America's Next Top Model*?" Gina snorted. "Uh-oh."

"Be quiet." Cassidy stepped forward.

THREE

Katie's plan was to sit at the bar and wait for someone to hit on her. Even if it was only the bartender, it would provide just the ego boost she needed to get through the night.

Walking along Macdougal, the first hint of September chill hit her shoulders, and she reveled in the sensation. Now, where was that wine bar again? Had she missed it? She could have sworn it was right here. She'd just pulled out her phone to try Googling it when she heard:

"Hope you're not checking your work email."

That voice. That startling female baritone.

Katie turned around expecting the suit, the shiny oxfords, the words *Falcon cannot agree to that.*

But it wasn't her.

Or wait.

It was her, but she looked different somehow—more relaxed and rugged in a casual button-down, dark jeans, and
leather boots, which appeared to be men's boots. She was
with a friend, an adorable little creature with tattoos and a
tiny fauxhawk that cut across the top of her (or his?) head
like a mini shark fin.

"Cassidy Price," Katie said.

"You remember me." Cassidy gave Katie a cocky smile.

How could I not? Katie wanted to say. But she kept her
mouth shut.

"You look good," Cassidy said, which Katie found wildly
inappropriate. "You must be going someplace special."

"I thought I was, but I think it's gone."

"You talking about the wine bar used to be here?" the little shark said in an accent that was more Mississippi than a
mud pie. "It's that luxury soap store now. They got soap in
there that looks so much like a cupcake I once snuck a lick
just to make sure."

"Huh," Katie said.

"Name's Gina." Sharkie put out her hand.

Katie returned the handshake, trying to mind her manners in spite of Cassidy's doing the whole aggressive-eye-
contact thing she'd pulled on Katie all day long.

"Were you meeting someone?" Cassidy asked.

Katie knew the correct answer was yes. But why should she lie? There was nothing wrong with enjoying some alone time on a Tuesday night.

"I just thought a nice glass of cabernet would do me good," Katie said in the voice of her chicest self. "After a difficult day at work."

Cassidy let out a measured laugh. "Well, there's certainly no cabernet to be found there." She pointed to the iridescent storefront. "Only soap you may confuse for dessert."

Katie forced a smile. Could this moment get any more awkward?

"Do you want to come out with us?" Cassidy asked.

Yup, this *could* get more awkward.

"Oh no, thanks, but I can't," Katie said.

Cassidy maintained eye contact. "Why not?"

"Because. I can't." Katie matched her forcefulness level to Cassidy's.

"You scared?" Gina said.

Of course Katie was scared. These were not her people. Would it be a gay bar they would take her to? It had to be, right? The closest Katie had ever come to stepping foot into a gay bar was the time she accidentally went for lunch at that restaurant where all the waitresses were drag queens.

"Come out for one drink," Cassidy said. "On me. I feel like I owe you that much after giving you hell all morning."

"That's nice of you but totally not necessary," Katie said, trying to keep this professional.

"Come on," Cassidy insisted. "Look at you. You're all dressed up; you look like you could use a little fun tonight."

Fun. Now, that was something Katie hadn't experienced in its purest form in a very long time. Paul Michael had recently taken her to a gallery called Phun with a "Ph," but that wasn't quite the same thing.

Still, though.

"Maybe some other time," Katie said. "Tonight I need some quiet time alone."

Cassidy looked down at her boots. "Okay then," she said. "Nice seeing you. Till tomorrow, I guess."

"Later, gator," Gina said.

They walked away, and Katie tried to figure out her next move. She looked at her phone, and panic ensued. She didn't actually want to be alone tonight. Fun was what she really needed. Just plain fun that was free of irony and didn't involve getting hit on by some bartender or some other random dude. It was too soon for that. She needed fun without sexual pressure. Maybe even fun without men. And what was the worst that could happen?

"Hey!" Katie called out to them. "Hey, wait up."

They turned around simultaneously.

"One drink," she said. "Why not?"

Cassidy gave Gina a nudge in the arm as if to say, *I told you so.*

Catching up to them, Katie asked, "Where are we going?"

"The Met," Cassidy said.

"The museum?"

That brought a cackle out of Gina. "Metropolis," she said. "It's a bar."

"Well that sounds generic enough," Katie said, somewhat relieved.

"What were you expecting?" Gina asked. "The Clit Club? Panty Hoes?"

Cassidy cracked up then—the first time Katie had ever heard a genuine laugh out of her, which she assumed meant Gina was messing with her.

"Tonight's Metropolis's Tuesday-night party," Cassidy said. "It's called Cunt Power."

"Oh," Katie said, unsure if she was messing with her now.

-ᏉᏉᏉ-

The moment Katie stepped into Metropolis—the Met—she noticed the soles of her Dior heels were sticking to the floor. She hadn't experienced a sticky barroom floor in years, and she hadn't missed it. The second thing she noticed was everyone else noticing her. Katie filed in just behind Cassidy, and she could almost hear the record scratch as everyone's attention turned toward them.

Was that her imagination?

First sight of the place was not what she was expecting. She thought it would be a little frightening and intimidating, that the faces turning to her might look downright angry, hard in the eyes, tight around the mouth. Muscle shirts, military buzz cuts, that sort of thing. But it wasn't like that at all. Plenty of these women looked like women— she spied a few other dresses in the crowd—and the ones who didn't look like women looked like *boys*. Not men. It was hard to be intimidated by a five-foot-two college kid wearing a flannel from Gap Kids.

The room was dimly lit, painted red. It smelled a little bit like cheese, but there was no cheese in sight. To the left of the entrance was the bar, lined with vinyl stools, where girls of all sizes and colors were crowding in on one another, waving cash at the bartender, who had a pink streak in her hair. Some of these girls had choppy asymmetrical haircuts and pierced noses; some were in short-shorts with tube socks pulled up to their knees. Many of them had forgotten to put on a bra before leaving the house. The girls who looked like boys wore skinny neckties or faded T-shirts with jeans that hung low off their hips. A few of them reminded Katie of Justin Bieber before he grew muscles.

"I think I'm a little overdressed for this place," Katie said to Cassidy over the music—which she was pretty sure was Joan Jett, circa 1981.

"You're dressed just right," Cassidy said. "Trust me."

"Yeah," said Gina. "There's a scarcity of femmes around here in case you haven't noticed."

"I don't even really know what that means," Katie said. "But I sense you aren't talking about film noir."

"Girly-girls," Gina said. "Lipstick lesbians."

"I'm not a femme," Katie said.

"You sure as hell ain't butch," Gina replied.

"No," Katie said. "Of course not." She wanted to elaborate further, to explain how she was neither, that she was just a normal, regular girl and that coming here was purely circumstantial. But before she had the chance, Cassidy took her by the hand and led her through the crowd toward the condensed group jostling for the bartender's attention.

"What can I get you to drink?" Cassidy asked.

Katie hesitated, and Cassidy added, "You don't want the cabernet. Trust me."

"Wild Turkey then," she said. "Neat."

Cassidy blinked her long dark eyelashes at Katie, quiet for a second. Then she said, "Huh."

"What does 'huh' mean?"

"Nothing."

"What? Were you expecting me to order something a little more weak?"

"No," Cassidy said. "A little more pink."

"Fuck off."

"Whoa." Gina smacked Cassidy on the back. "That came even sooner in the night than I expected."

"Really?" Katie peered down at Gina, gripping her hands to her hips. "Because I've been wanting to tell her to fuck off since around nine thirty this morning." It occurred to Katie then that she'd already had a good amount of Wild Turkey at her apartment, or she wouldn't have come out and said something so rudely honest. One more drink was definitely all she could handle.

Gina did an about-face. "I'm gonna go get on the pool table list."

Katie went to follow behind her, but Gina zipped through the crowd so fast she immediately lost track of her, so instead Katie stayed put, waiting for Cassidy to wrangle their drinks.

Katie tried to look like she belonged in the space she was occupying, to not stare at anyone, but she'd never experienced a place like this before. Just off to her right two girls were making out so aggressively she was afraid one of them might lose a tongue. They were both wearing blue hoodies and Converse sneakers, and both had short bleached-blond hair. In fact, they could have passed for twin gender-neutral siblings if Katie hadn't known better. This baffled her, because if this world was supposedly made up of femmes and butches, what were these two? And was this sort of hooking up with your own doppelgänger frowned upon or championed?

While Katie was pondering this, a woman approached her. She herself didn't blend; she was older than the mostly twentysomething crowd by a solid decade and style-wise was dressed more for, say, hitting up a golf tournament than a night of cruising for girls. She was wearing a black fleece jacket that was zipped all the way up and pleated khaki shorts that hit just above her knees. She might have had a perm; Katie couldn't really tell because she was also wearing a white ball cap with mirrored Oakley sunglasses resting on top of the cap's bill.

"Can I buy you a drink?" the woman asked.

Oh god.

"Thanks, but my friend is getting me one." Katie pointed toward the bar, hoping to divert this person's attention, but instead she continued staring directly into Katie's eyes.

"You're new here, aren't you?" she said. "You must be, because if you'd been here before I'd remember."

This was all too much. Katie needed to either take a breath or vomit. "Excuse me," Katie said, and then disappeared herself into the crowd, searching for the restroom.

It was all the way in the back, in a dark corner, of course. Katie assumed it was unisex because the signage on the door was a chalk drawing of a stick figure with very big hair, giant boobs, and an equally giant penis.

She knocked pointlessly, checked to make sure the pro golfer hadn't followed her, and then pushed open the door using only her knuckles. Inside were two stalls, one with a door and one— "Oh, pardon me," she said.

Two women were going at it inside the doorless stall in a way Katie thought only happened on Xtube. One of them had her back to Katie—a harmless enough white T-shirt and blue jeans—but the other one was all skin and leg meat. Her thigh was flexibly suspended over the T-shirted one's shoulder.

They didn't acknowledge Katie, and rather than repeat her apology for the intrusion, she opted for the stall with a door. To her horror, though, the door had no lock. Also, one look at the toilet paper roll and it was obvious to Katie that it had previously fallen into the toilet and been fished out. But she really did have to pee, so she did her best to not touch anything and tried to keep calm by reading the walls. There she found the usual hearts and arrows. *SlutWhore Wuz Here. MJB gives great head. I hate that bitch. Fuck U Ho. You have HPV.*

Boy had this night taken a turn. If that wine bar had simply been where it was supposed to be, Katie would probably have had the bartender's phone number by now and she'd have been using a restroom with one of those bamboo air diffusers that made everything smell like citrus. Instead she was here drip-drying on account of the toilet paper situation, certain she was about to contract a staph infection.

To the left of the missing door lock, Katie noticed a numbered list of names in hot-pink block letters. *Best Fucks List.* Cassidy was listed at number two, beneath a girl named Dana, but then someone had crossed out Dana's name and written Cassidy on top, which then prompted a few others to weigh in: *Biggest Slut! Total Playa!* Someone else had written, *Totes worth it tho!*

So it appeared that Cassidy Price was something of a cad. Hardly the hero Katie had witnessed earlier in the boardroom. She had to wonder then if Cassidy's eagerness to get her to join them tonight was more than a simple gesture of goodwill. Did the *total playa* think she could get her into bed?

And, oh Christ, one of the young women in the stall beside hers was reaching orgasm, she was pretty sure. Katie had to get the hell out of here. She had to chug that drink waiting for her without touching her lips to the glass if possible, and then get herself back home to her couch. No, even before the couch she would take a shower. A long, hot, steaming, cleansing shower.

Katie exited the bathroom rubbing her palms with the peach-scented hand sanitizer she kept in her purse.

"Check out Miss Priss over here," someone called out, followed by a round of mean female laughter.

"This one's got to be one of Cassidy's," someone else said.

Katie frantically searched the room and caught sight of Gina's shark fin at the pool table. She was chalking up a cue. Then Katie saw Cassidy carrying their drinks from the bar toward the two empty stools near the corner of the pool table. She caught Katie's eye and nodded at the stools with her chin.

When Katie reached her, Cassidy handed her one of the glasses, and Katie immediately swallowed down a healthy sip.

Cassidy settled onto the red leatherette stool beside hers like it was her favorite living-room recliner. She stretched her long legs out in front of her and crossed her boots at the ankles. "So what do you think?" she asked. "Have you ever been to a place like this before?"

"I've been to dives way worse than this," Katie said. "You should see my hometown."

"Not what I meant."

Cassidy was smiling, so Katie smiled, and while smiling she said, "Just to be clear, you know I'm straight, right?"

Cassidy laughed, then folded her arms over the chest of her chambray button-down, which was tailored as smartly as her work shirt had been but was untucked for a more casual effect. "That's why I thought this might be your first dyke bar," Cassidy said.

"Oh. It is," Katie replied matter-of-factly.

"So, then, what do you think?"

Katie scanned the space, hoping not to lock eyes with the pro golfer or those bitches who'd laughed at her because of her sanitizer.

"No offense," Katie said, "but aren't there any nicer lesbian bars?"

"Not really." Cassidy uncrossed her ankles. "Well, there are some, but they're not the Met."

Gina looked up over her pool cue. "That's a lie. There's plenty of fancy places with clean glasses and girls Cassidy's own age. But she prefers 'em young and dirty."

"Speaks highly of you," Katie said.

Cassidy shrugged, unapologetic.

"How old *are* you?" Katie asked.

"Probably about the same age as you."

"I'm twenty-eight," Katie said.

"Me too."

"She's thirty," Gina called out, just before sinking three balls with one shot.

"You came on a good night." Cassidy pretended she hadn't just been caught lying about her age. "You're going to see all our best celesbians." She pointed with her bourbon glass. "See that girl over there? You recognize her?"

The woman Cassidy had gestured toward was black with a shaved head and had the most beautiful smile Katie had ever seen on anyone.

"That's Sabrina Weil," Cassidy said. "She's a model.

There's a giant billboard of her in her underwear in Times Square right now. And the girl standing next to her, that's Chef Becky. Have you seen that cooking show *Knife Fight*? Becky was on season three, but she lost."

Gina stood up straight at the sound of Chef Becky's name, planting her pool cue hard at her side. "Becky used to be a vegan. She's got a goddamn vegan tattoo across her stomach. Right here." She indicated her own belly. "Old English letters, v-e-g-a-n. And now she's famous for being a nose-to-tail butcher. One of these days I'm gonna call the TV station and tell them about that tattoo."

Cassidy whispered an explanation into Katie's ear. "Gina got her little heart butchered by the butcher once upon a time."

"My ex was a vegan," Katie said, in an effort at consolation that came out a few decibels too loud.

Gina, about to line up her next shot, paused. "So that means you're single, then?"

Katie pretended not to hear her and was quickly bailed out.

"Who's your friend, Cassidy?" The chef herself approached their corner.

"Katie Daniels," Cassidy said, "meet Chef Becky."

Becky was on the short side, adorably chubby in the exact way you want a chef to be, and she was wearing a purple bandana around her head.

She reached for Katie's hand, lifted it to her lips, and kissed it. "Pleasure to make your acquaintance. What are you drinking, honey?" She picked up Katie's empty glass and sniffed it. Then she lifted her arm and called out to the bartender with the pink stripe in her hair. "Dahlia, a round of whiskey shots over here!"

"Wow," Katie said. "You have a very impressive sense of smell."

"Oh, baby," Becky said. "You have no idea."

Cassidy gave Katie's elbow a little tug to pull her back from Becky's forward lean.

Quick to notice this move, Becky narrowed her eyes at Cassidy. "Oh, I see how it is. She's officially one of yours."

"I'm nobody's," Katie shot back. "And actually I think I should probably get going."

"Whaaaat? No," Becky said. "We've only just met."

"We have an early morning," Katie said to Cassidy.

"That's true," Cassidy said. "We do."

Except just then their shots arrived. Becky took one for herself and handed one to Katie. "Come on," she said. "Stick around for a bit."

The second Katie took that shot glass in hand she knew— if she drank it, she would be a goner. But down the hatch it went. Her brain fuzzed and the light dimmed, and she was feeling pretty frigging good then.

Soon an Asian girl with spiky hair and aggressive green

eye shadow, whose name Katie didn't catch, had her hand on Katie's back and was asking if she lived around here. She was saying something about the girl party she threw on the first Friday of every month, and drink tickets, something about how she would give Katie free drink tickets.

Then the model Cassidy had pointed out earlier crowded into their corner as well. Close up her skin looked so soft and smooth, she could have easily done commercials for Dove soap.

All the while, Cassidy stayed put at Katie's side, book-ending her with whoever this spiky-haired stranger was rubbing her back.

"You like to eat?" Chef Becky asked. "You eat meat?"

"She eats meat," Cassidy answered for her. "*Only* meat."

The model threw back her beautiful head and laughed, and Katie was sure the whole bar brightened. "We'll see about that," she said. Then she picked up Katie's empty glass. "What are you drinking?"

"Wild Turkey!" Chef Becky slammed her hand down on the edge of the pool table. "She drinks Wiiiiild Turkey! Because she is my kind of girl!"

"Hey, Chef," Cassidy said. "Take it down a notch."

"What?" Becky adjusted her bandana like she was gussy-ing up for a fight. "You think just 'cause you bring 'em, you own 'em? Well I think this young lady is free roaming, just like the chickens on my sustainable farm upstate. Am I right, Katie?"

Katie nodded in agreement, because how could she not?

Becky raised her glass. "She's meant to run wild!"

The others raised their glasses in accord.

Katie sort of couldn't believe any of what was happening. There was literally a circle of women around her, and every single one of them was hitting on her. They were practically fighting over her! And these were the celesbians. They must have been, like, the elite of their world.

Katie found herself giggling, electrified by the attention. If this were a group of men she might have felt overwhelmed, threatened, even. If it were just one man crowding her with such a blatant attempt at seduction, she would have gotten the hell out of there faster than you could say *rape whistle*. But this felt harmless rather than predatory, and even the way Cassidy had positioned herself at Katie's side, like her own personal bodyguard, struck Katie as amusing.

At some point they all just started calling Katie "Wild Turkey." Instead of *What are you drinking?* it became *Wild Turkey, you ready for another?*

The Asian girl with the spiky hair had worked her arm all the way around Katie's torso and was holding her so close she could smell her cologne. Katie was way taller than she was, definitely stronger, and could have easily pulled away, but the closeness felt good, safe somehow.

Chef Becky went on about the restaurant she was opening in DUMBO. ". . . I am talking whole hog. Nothing will go to waste. Ears, tail, we'll serve old Porky's head right there on a bed of mustard greens."

The model, whatever her name was, was more on the quiet side. She let her million-dollar smile do most of her bragging for her. But then her girlfriend showed up, and she stopped smiling so much and sulked away into the crowd.

Becky jumped at the opening of having one less competitor. "What do you say you and me go out back for some fresh air?" she asked.

"There's a backyard here?" Katie asked.

"Nope." Cassidy grabbed Katie by the hand. She pulled her free from the spiky-haired stranger's hold and Becky's forward lean and escorted her through the crowd to the other end of the bar.

"Is somebody jealous of all the attention I'm getting?" Katie said, but Cassidy ignored her.

Katie thought Cassidy might be taking her to the backyard herself, but instead they stopped at a game machine called Megatouch that looked like something out of the eighties movie *Big*.

Cassidy shoved a dollar into the machine, and its screen came to light. She chose a game called Erotic Photo Hunt, which was simple enough to follow. It was basically the same game as the one in the back of the tabloids, except you had to find the differences between two nearly identical pictures of scantily clad women. The women were posed explicitly in otherwise innocent places like backyard barbecues and holiday-themed dining rooms.

"I don't get jealous," Cassidy said in a delayed response to Katie's allegation. She tapped at the screen's dissimilar flower pots and areolas. "I assumed I was doing you a favor."

"Oh please," Katie said. "It's not like I would actually—"

"Hey, Dahlia," Cassidy said, cutting Katie off, calling out over her shoulder. "Can you send over a glass of water? A big one. Maybe a pitcher."

"It's cute that you're worried about me," Katie said. "But I'm fine. I'm having a blast. I'm so happy you brought me here."

"Glad to hear it," Cassidy said. "But it is getting late. Probably a good idea to start winding down."

"Why *did* you bring me here?" Katie asked.

Cassidy turned from the screen for a moment to look at Katie straight on. Her features were bathed in the machine's erotic hot-pink glow. "I'm not sure what you're asking me. You were alone. It was the polite thing to do."

"Do you really have such good manners?" Katie got too close to the machine and accidentally brushed up against a spot that made Cassidy lose the game.

"Probably not as good as yours." Cassidy slipped another dollar into the machine and began again. "Where'd you grow up? Somewhere in the South?"

"Kentucky," Katie said, and then hiccupped.

"That explains your accent."

"I don't have an accent."

"You sure do, Wild Turkey. And it gets heavier with every drink."

"Well so do you," Katie said. "You have the accent of New York coastal elitism. Let me guess, you were born and raised in Manhattan, private schooled. Your parents are probably both doctors."

Cassidy cracked a half smile but said nothing.

"I'm right, aren't I?"

"No," Cassidy said. "Only my father is a doctor. My mother's an artist."

Katie lost it then. "Ha! I knew it. Wait, wait, what kind of artist? Does she, like, throw paint or sit in public and stare?"

Cassidy turned away from her game and looked down at the filthy floor. "She's really into traffic cones right now, like putting eyes on them."

"Oh my god, I totally know her work." Katie leaned all the way against the Megatouch machine now. "My ex-fiancé was a curator. So I know all about that crap."

Cassidy eyed Katie cautiously. "What happened?"

"He dumped me for my best friend. Like three days ago."

"I mean, how did you, Katie the Wild Turkey from Kentucky, end up a corporate lawyer engaged to a New York curator?"

"Exactly," Katie said, just as Dahlia appeared with their water.

Katie accepted the glass from Dahlia and then handed it off to Cassidy. "I don't want this. Let's do another shot instead."

"Absolutely not," Cassidy said, but the next thing Katie remembered was doing another shot—and then dancing. Which was interesting because there wasn't a dance floor at Metropolis. There was, however, Pat Benatar, or something equally awesome and ridiculous, ringing in her ears.

The rest was a blur of hands and hair and perfumed hot skin and sweat.

At some point Katie fell down. And someone—possibly Dahlia?—said, *Get this drunk-ass bitch out of here.*

Then it was Cassidy's arms.

A cab.

Where do you live?

Katie recited her address, but it was the wrong address—the one to Paul Michael's SoHo condo—so she course-corrected them to the right address, but was crying, then sobbing. *I don't even know where I live anymore!*

Katie remembered the front door to her apartment. Cassidy losing her patience. *Which key, Katie? Which key is it?*

"I don't know. I don't know!"

Finally they were inside Katie's apartment—the right one, in the West Village, with all the cardboard moving boxes strewn about.

Off with her shoes, and maybe her dress?

It was hazy, what happened next, but Katie distinctly remembered how sweetly Cassidy cared for her and how she carted Katie to the bathroom—fortuitous on her part, because they made it to the toilet just in time.

Katie couldn't remember anything after that.

FOUR

Cassidy helped Katie into her building and up the four
flights of stairs to her apartment because the likelihood of
her wiping out and cracking her face open on the stairwell
was much too great. She'd planned to turn right around and
make her escape the moment Katie was safely inside, but
curiosity took over once she laid eyes on the place. She followed Katie into the foul-smelling living room, stepping
over cardboard boxes and empty food containers. A plastic
bag that doubled for a trash can overflowed with Kleenex.

Cassidy remembered then, about the ex-fiancé, and it all
started to make sense. This apartment was a disaster—Katie
was a disaster—because she was in pain.

"Do you need anything?" Cassidy asked. "Before I go?"

Katie shimmied off her dress and stepped out of it.

Cassidy averted her eyes, but it was too late. She'd already
seen Katie's silky black bra and underwear.

"Please don't go." Katie came closer, wrapped her arms around Cassidy's neck. "I'm all alone."

In spite of herself, Cassidy felt something—a weakening of her defenses now that Katie's sadness was so evident.

"You're not alone." She made no effort to remove Katie's forearms from where they were resting upon her shoulders. "You're going to be okay."

"I really like you," Katie said, and then hiccupped. She brought her face in close to Cassidy's, and Cassidy knew she couldn't kiss her. She was disgusted with herself for wanting to, for the momentary deliberation.

Then Katie's face changed.

"You okay?" Cassidy asked.

Katie bolted for the bathroom and made it to the toilet just in time.

Christ. Cassidy had to look away. What the hell was she doing here?

She went to the kitchen to get Katie a glass of water and was taken aback all over again by the overturned liquor bottles littering the counter and kitchen table. She would have mistaken it all for a Labor Day party's aftermath if she didn't know better.

Against her better judgment she opened the fridge. It was empty of food, as she expected, but at least it wasn't stock-piled with booze. Closing the door, she noticed a few faded photos stuck with magnets to its front.

Cassidy reached for the most adorable of the bunch, a

photo of Katie as a little girl perched upon a horse. She looked like a real-life American Girl doll, big blue eyes, shiny blond braid, complete with mini equestrian outfit and tiny riding helmet.

Beside that was a family photo, the posed kind, where everyone was in color-coordinated outfits. Katie and her mother were in dresses; her father and two brothers were in ties. Katie was the youngest and she couldn't have been a day over fifteen when this was taken, but without a hint of the pubescent awkwardness that Cassidy had suffered at that age. They were a handsome, wholesome group—the father hulking over the rest of them like a good-natured bear; the mother with a hint of protective concern behind her stiff smile; a wiliness to the brothers, who were close in age and no doubt sportsmen. They were a regular family in the way that triggered Cassidy's basest resentments. She couldn't help but be suspicious of any group that fit so seamlessly in this world, at least on the surface.

It wasn't cool, and certainly not PC, to admit that the sight of Katie's brothers sent a chill up Cassidy's spine. They stirred in her a volatile mixture of fear and aggression, these boys-will-be-boys kind of men. She could almost see the other photos in a family album somewhere, of the two of them bullet-belted, toting rifles, flashing huge grins over some enormous dead animal. They were the kind of guys Cassidy would cross the street to avoid because her intolerance of them was palpable, yes, but also in fear they'd attack her for sport, too, if she came too close.

Another photo on the fridge was of Katie arm in arm with a group of girls, all wearing college sweatshirts. Some of the sweatshirts were bright orange and read *University of Tennessee*; others read *University of Hard Knox*. There were sweatshirts that brandished Greek letters or a red-and-yellow crest. Katie's was gray with burgundy lettering: *Chi Omega, Since 1895*. Cassidy stepped back to take in the group as a whole. So much blond hair and fair skin and light eyes. Perfect-looking girls with perfect little lives.

Farther down the fridge door, Cassidy found a more recent photo of what had to be Katie and her ex-fiancé. They were dressed in formal attire, probably at someone's wedding. She looked happy, Katie did. He looked like a dipshit, so normal it was nauseating, but Katie seemed to really like him, at least in this picture.

Cassidy turned away from the photos then, and without thinking she began tidying up. She gathered the empty over-turned liquor bottles on the counter into a garbage bag and piled a few sticky mugs into the sink. She checked the coffeemaker, chucked out the old filter, and filled a fresh one with the container of Folgers beside the machine.

Cassidy didn't even know this girl. Why did she care if she had coffee in the morning? Why was she drawn to this mess?

In the cabinet, Cassidy found a clean glass and filled it

with water. She walked it to the bedroom, where she found Katie facedown on her mattress.

"Katie?" she said from the doorway.

She could at least tell Katie was breathing by the slight rise and fall of her black bra and underwear. As she stepped closer, to set the glass of water onto the nightstand, she could also hear her snoring.

Cassidy thought to cover her with a blanket but was too afraid to touch her. Instead, she checked to make sure Katie's alarm clock was set and then quietly made her escape.

Headphones on, music blaring, Cassidy tried to shake off all memories of the previous night. She upped her speed and her treadmill's incline to physically run them out of her mind. She could not go into work distracted today. She had to be business as usual. Get in, close this deal, and get out. Then Katie Daniels would be a thing of the past. She would likely never see her again.

Cassidy imagined herself later that night joking about it over drinks with Gina and Becky. Dahlia would reenact how she had to come out from behind the bar to help drag the straight-girl shit-show out to the curb.

Someone would no doubt ask, *Did you hook up with her?*

Yeah, she'd reply sarcastically. *Because I'm a date rapist. Of course I didn't hook up with her!*

But are you going to see her again?

God no, Cassidy would say. *Once was more than enough!*
She pictured how they'd laugh at this part, how she'd buy
everyone a round, and that would be that.

So why the hell was she running, literally sprinting, at
twice the normal speed this morning? Like she wanted her
heart to burst from her chest.

Those photos on Katie's refrigerator door had gotten to
her; they'd stirred a strange and familiar longing.

Cassidy had woken up thinking of Monica—of the
first time they lay together with their hips touching, legs
entwined, and how afterward they smoked a cigarette like
they'd seen couples do in the movies but pretended nothing
unusual had just gone on. It was a well-worn memory that
came to Cassidy only in moments of weakness, unfurling
against her will to all that followed—how junior year Monica started dating Noah Cooper, and how senior year Cassidy found herself in the sickening position of documenter at
pre-prom pictures.

After all these years and countless women, innumera-
ble humiliations erased and conquered, this one persisted,
harbored malevolently in the walls of Cassidy's mind like a
haunting.

"You're going to come see us off, aren't you?" Monica
had said. "You have to come! You always take the best pictures of me."

It was true that Cassidy had been incapable of taking a bad photo of Monica, because for Cassidy taking a photo of Monica was a flash of perfection. It was Monica's shape and form suspended in place, where if she came back in an hour to check, this Monica would remain exactly as she was, still smiling back at her as proof of something.

Monica's prom dress was rose quartz—Cassidy would never forget it. It was a color she'd had difficulty visualizing when Monica described it. But seeing it on Monica that afternoon, Cassidy understood how it wasn't simply pink, as she'd suspected; it was in fact the exact hue of a crystallized gemstone transmitting a pale pink light.

After watching their limo drive away, Cassidy walked home in the opposite direction, hands dug deep into her jeans pockets, head down.

"Are you sorry now?" her mother had said when she arrived home. "Are you sorry you're not going? Now that you saw how nice everyone looked and how happy they all were?"

Cassidy slowed her treadmill's pace and reduced her incline before she actually did have a heart attack. She wiped the sweat from her face with her towel.

Shake it off, she told herself. Shake it off. Stay present. Focus on the task at hand.

But are you going to see her again?

God no, she would say. *Once was more than enough!*

FIVE

Katie woke up to her head blaring like an ambulance and her mouth as dry as week-old bread. There was a full glass of water on her nightstand and she chugged it down, then got herself into the shower.

What had she done? And, worse, how was she supposed to face Cassidy now, all day long, with her *Falcon cannot agree to that* bullshit?

Katie stepped out of the shower needing coffee so badly she could almost smell it. No, wait, she was definitely smelling it. This was no hallucination, but how was that possible?

Sure enough, her coffeemaker had prepared her a steaming four-cup pot. So either she had set up the machine and set its timer in a blackout (unlikely) or Cassidy had done it before leaving last night. It was an act of heartfelt thoughtfulness that made having to go head-to-head with her this morning slightly less mortifying. But only slightly.

Katie drank her first cup of coffee while digging through the hallway closet just outside her bathroom—what she believed was intended to be a linen closet but in an apartment this small was more like a linen closet/medicine cabinet/ storage cupboard. It contained every household item that couldn't fit anywhere else. Bath towels, dish towels, toilet paper, random appliances she'd purchased on a whim and used only once, like a salad spinner. Katie was searching for antacid, but wouldn't you know it—she found an iron. It would have been awesome if she'd stumbled upon it yesterday, but she was not about to look a gift iron in the mouth.

Katie kicked a few boxes from the center of the living room floor in order to lay down a towel and iron her black skirt suit. It was a different black skirt suit from yesterday, but only if you looked closely. She'd wear it with a cream-colored blouse today instead of white.

While ironing her suit to perfection she tried to recall how exactly she had gone from screwing up Cassidy's Mega-touch game last night to ending up with her here at her apartment. And why in the world did she take off her dress?

She dragged an IKEA chair from the kitchen into her bedroom, then slid her nightstand in front of the mirror to construct a makeshift vanity. It was not quite the handcrafted, beveled-glass makeup nook she'd grown accustomed to in SoHo, but it would do.

With her face nearly knocking into the mirror, Katie applied a yellow-tinted concealer to the dark circles under her eyes and then lined them with a neutral pencil to counteract their redness. Her face was coming together, but Cassidy Price had still seen her in nothing but her underwear. This fact was undeniable. Katie had never before been met with the predicament of heading into a negotiation where opposing counsel knew beyond a shadow of a doubt that her belly button was an innie, but she was fairly certain it put her at a disadvantage.

When she arrived at the Falcon Capital building, she stepped out of her cab and locked eyes with Cassidy, who was—of course—stepping out of the car directly in front of hers.

Katie forced herself to hold Cassidy's gaze. She could not succumb to the shame. "Hey," she said, immediately realizing how flippant it came out sounding. Good, she thought. Go with that. She brought even more levity to her voice. "Did you set my coffeemaker last night?"

For whatever reason, Katie's posing this question caused Cassidy to blush. "Yeah," she said, like it was no big deal.

"That was very nice of you." Katie chuckled. "I have to say, no man would have done that."

Cassidy laughed uncomfortably and then gestured to the building's front door. "Shall we?"

Katie let Cassidy hold the door open for her, and they rode the elevator together in total silence. Katie swore she could smell Wild Turkey emitting from her pores but willed herself to ignore it. She told herself that Cassidy should be just as embarrassed as she was right now because Cassidy was the one spending her nights fucking twenty-two-year-olds in a filthy girl-bar bathroom. What would Falcon think about that? Katie doubted very much Falcon would agree to that.

The two of them entered the conference room and separated to opposite sides of the table.

"Let's get started," Katie's boss said. "We have a lot to cover if we want to close today."

They proceeded much the same way as the day before. We want this but they want this, you claim this but they think this, yada yada yada.

Katie and Cassidy were seated across from each other just as they had been yesterday, but today instead of trying to imagine Cassidy's life, Katie was straining to push it out of her mind. She didn't want to have a mental picture of Cassidy searching and pecking through a game of erotic photo hunt, or of her ragtag group of friends, or, worst of all, her ranking on the Best Fucks List.

In fact, Katie had to question Ms. Price's judgment for allowing her to see all of that. Why would someone who relied so heavily on intimidation in the boardroom, aggressive

eye contact, and a $300 haircut give her such an unadulter-
ated view of her underside?

As they negotiated back and forth, Cassidy's recurring
Falcon cannot agree to that sounded less maddening to Katie's ears. Not quite so brash or arrogant. And in spite of
Katie's throbbing head and nausea, she was on top of her
legal game, so much so that she believed it was clear to everyone at the table that the power balance had shifted in her
team's direction.

Perhaps having Cassidy see her in her underwear last
night had put her at the disadvantage instead of Katie.
Even so, when the deal was done—miraculously by around
eight p.m. that night—Katie made a quick round of handshakes before dashing to the ladies' room, where she planned
to hide until Cassidy went home.

That's where Cassidy found her, leaning against the sink,
gazing at her own shamefaced reflection.

"I thought you might be in here," Cassidy said.

Katie pretended like she needed to wash her hands.

"Good work today," Cassidy said.

"Thanks." Katie used way more soap than necessary and
took her sweet time scrubbing each finger individually in
hopes that Cassidy would head into a stall, allowing her to
make her escape.

But Cassidy stayed put.

Katie turned off the faucet and shook out her hands because it was inconceivable that she could continue washing them any longer. Then she pivoted away from Cassidy to reach for one, two, three paper towels.

While Cassidy watched her thoroughly dry her hands, Katie thought maybe she was just bad at goodbyes. Their deal was done. This would likely be the last time they'd ever see each other. Maybe on account of the craziness of last night Cassidy felt like she owed Katie a friendlier farewell than the abrupt handshake they'd already exchanged. But as far as Katie was concerned, they'd spent more than enough time on this tête-à-tête. It was time to end this.

Katie picked up her purse and her briefcase from where she'd set them down on the window's ledge. "Look," she said. "I'm sorry about last night. I'm not usually such a hot mess. I just got out of a bad breakup, and I was feeling—"

"It's cool. You don't have to apologize." Cassidy was looking every which way now, every which way except right at Katie. "You were loads of fun last night. You made yourself many fans."

Okay then, Katie was about to say when Cassidy shocked her by asking, "Do you want to grab some dinner?"

"I can't," Katie reflexively shot back. "I have plans." Which was a lie. She was in fact starving and dreading going back to her empty apartment alone.

"Well, let me give you my number." Cassidy took out her phone.

"Oh, no," Katie said. "I don't . . . I'm not. I mean, I won't . . ."

Cassidy halted, then put her phone back into her suit pocket. She scratched at the back of her neck. "At least take this." Cassidy pulled out a business card. "My cell's on there if . . ."

Katie took the card from Cassidy's fingers but didn't give it so much as a glance. She didn't offer her one of hers.

Cassidy backed off then, finally, and turned to leave without saying goodbye.

"Take care," Katie said as the bathroom door swung soundlessly closed behind her.

Katie knew she had hurt Cassidy's feelings, but that was just too frigging bad. Better than giving her the wrong idea. What did she think Katie was? Just because she got a little drunk and made a fool of herself.

Then the bathroom door swung back open and Cassidy reappeared. "You know, I'm not hitting on you," she said. "You don't have to be such a snob. It's just dinner."

Katie was stunned for a second by Cassidy's forwardness. She said, "I'm not a snob. You are."

"Very mature." Cassidy smiled.

"Fine," Katie said. "I could use some dinner. Where to?"

SIX

The moment their waitress set down a plate of complimentary pâté Cassidy knew she was doomed. She'd accepted that there was a chance Raquel would be in the kitchen tonight, but she'd chanced it because this restaurant was the ideal place to take Katie for dinner. It had just the right atmosphere for them to sit and have a nice meal and partake in meaningful conversation, a perfect balance of edge and intimacy. Some might have called it the ideal date restaurant—unless, like Cassidy, you'd slept with the chef for a few weeks, then promptly stopped answering her texts once she broke up with her girlfriend to be with you.

"The chef here is a friend," Cassidy said, in explanation for the free pâté.

A moment later Raquel appeared wearing checkered chef

pants and a black skullcap over her asymmetrical bangs. She set down an artistically arranged beet salad and then gave Katie a pointed once-over.

Katie returned the favor, observing Raquel's pierced labret and tattooed forearms.

"Hi." Raquel extended her hand to Katie. "I'm Raquel."

"Hello," Katie said. "Nice to meet you."

"You ladies here for dinner?" she asked.

"Yeah," Cassidy said. "I was thinking—"

Raquel cut her off. "I've got you. I know what you like, Cassidy." Raquel shot a malevolent glance at Katie and then raised her eyebrows at Cassidy. "You want it raw tonight?"

Before Cassidy could get a word out, Raquel turned back toward the kitchen. Over her shoulder she said loud enough for the whole place to hear, "I hope your friend eats fish."

Cassidy cleared her throat. "Just to clarify, she was referring to the crudo. The raw—"

Katie held up her hand to make Cassidy stop talking.

The wine they ordered arrived, and Cassidy was thankful to have hers. She took a long sip.

"Let me guess," Katie said. "You used to date Chef Raquel."

Cassidy tapped at the side of her wineglass. "*Date* is a strong word."

"Not really."

"It's more like we've shared a few special moments."

"I see. So should I worry about the pâté being poisoned?"

"Maybe you should let me taste it first." Cassidy dug into the pâté then, and scooped them each some beet salad. "She's a friend of Becky's. That's how I know her."

One bite of beets and Cassidy's head spun. She was hungrier than she'd realized.

"I had no idea there were so many lesbian chefs in this town." Katie seemed choke on the word *lesbian*, but she tried to save it by adding, "I'm kind of fascinated by your life. You seem to really know how to have a good time."

"If last night was any indication," Cassidy said, "you do have some idea of how to let your hair down."

"Please don't bring up last night ever again."

"Sorry. Didn't mean to make light of it." Cassidy jumped at the opportunity to steer the conversation away from herself. "It seems like you're going through a rough time. With your breakup and all."

Katie nodded. "I think last night at the bar I was trying to feel like somebody else. For once in my life to be completely careless and carefree."

"Hear, hear." Cassidy raised her glass. "Careless and carefree happens to be my specialty. See? We are meant to be friends."

Katie pushed some beets around her plate with her fork. Her face was opalescent in the light from their table's flickering candle.

Cassidy was breaking her own rules, contradicting herself by just being here. She was supposed to bid Katie goodbye today, and instead they were sitting across from a table together, alone, and she was leaning too far forward, hopped up and overeager.

They were interrupted then by a special delivery from the kitchen—an enormous two-tiered plate of oysters, mussels, clams, shrimp, and tuna tartare.

"Wow," Katie said. "Raquel was not messing around. There is a whole lot of raw, vaguely vaginic seafood before us."

Cassidy squeezed some lemon onto an oyster and slurped it down. "I'm pretty sure *vaginic* isn't a word."

"It's not?" Katie went for a shrimp, probably because it was less suggestive. "Well it should be."

It had been hours since either of them had eaten, and together they ravaged that plate. Cassidy watched Katie, hungry as she was, lost in the reverie of juice, flavor, wine.

Behind Katie a wall was painted with quotations from Ernest Hemingway, Henry Miller, and F. Scott Fitzgerald. Sentimental declarations on food, enjoyment, sucking the marrow—the kind of thing Cassidy would normally scoff at as trying too hard, but tonight they struck her as a seamless backdrop to Katie's iridescence.

Katie leaned across the table and brought her voice down like she had a secret. "Can I ask you something personal?"

Cassidy waited, sensing they were on the brink of something.

"Were you always this way?"

Cassidy paused midbite to smile crookedly. "Do you mean was I always this awesome?"

"I mean, this." Katie waved her fork at Cassidy. "Were you prancing around the halls of your high school wearing custom suits and hitting on girls in the locker room?"

"Not exactly. It wasn't until college that this"—Cassidy waved her own fork at herself as Katie had done—"happened."

She could pinpoint it to an exact moment, actually, during her first week at NYU when she'd been walking along Broome Street and that woman crossed in front of her—that woman who would never know the profound effect she had on young Cassidy's future. Like Cassidy, she was tall and slim with broad shoulders. She had the same dark hair, but hers was cut short and she wore a crisp dress shirt with a light scarf that flew behind her in the breeze. When she stepped to the corner and raised her hand to hail a cab, Cassidy quickly pulled out her phone and snapped a photo.

At the time Cassidy couldn't say why, but she studied the photo for a long while right there on the street. There was something about this stranger that she had the urge to memorize. She didn't look like a woman, exactly, and she didn't look like a man. But she looked good. Cassidy continued on, dazed, not entirely sure where she was going, until she found herself in front of a salon window. Through its slick glass, everyone inside looked like a model or an actress, but intimidating as this was, she forced herself to enter and approach the receptionist.

"Do you take walk-ins?" Cassidy had asked, having never hated her dark ponytail more than she did in that moment.

The skinny giraffe of a woman scoffed. "We schedule three months out."

But the tattooed woman behind her looked up. "I just had a cancellation. Have you been here before?"

"No." Cassidy held up her phone with the picture of the stranger. "But can you give me this haircut? I have money."

The tattooed woman squinted at the phone, then back at Cassidy. "Hot," she said. "Come on, let's get you washed."

The haircut turned out to be an outrageous three hundred dollars, but Cassidy considered it worth every penny, especially because she used her parents' credit card to pay for it. Back on the street she found herself newly capable of keeping her head up while she walked—a trait of contention her mother would have gladly forked over three hundred bucks to see corrected. She checked her reflection in every storefront she passed, reassessing herself from the neck down—her baggy hoodie, loose jeans, and torn-up Converse. She paused on the corner of Broome and Mercer, bowled over by the yearning to shop for new clothes.

She could almost hear her mother's incredulity in her ear. "But you hate shopping, Cassidy. You hate clothes!"

No. Young Cassidy observed the stylish panorama of well-groomed men wearing jackets and ties and tailored pants with superb chic. She didn't hate clothes. She hated clothes for girls.

Katie forked the last shrimp from their two-tiered plate and dipped it in cocktail sauce. "Were you straight before college?" Cassidy hesitated, and Katie set down her fork. "Sorry. Maybe that was rude to ask. I didn't mean to pry."

"Not at all." Cassidy wiped her mouth with her napkin. "I was just trying to think of the right answer." She gestured to their waitress for more wine. "I brought a girl home for the first time Thanksgiving of freshman year. Though I should clarify that by *home for Thanksgiving* I mean I brought a girl to the uptown restaurant where my parents rented a room each year to host the holiday."

"Only in New York," Katie said.

"Exactly. Stodgy venue, catered menu, and the enigmatic roster of my parents' friends who were a mix of doctors and artists."

Their wineglasses were refilled as Cassidy continued.

"When I arrived at the restaurant holding hands with this girl, I was wearing a sport coat, a button-down, designer jeans, and dress shoes, all from the men's department at Barneys. As expected, my mother gasped at the sight of me.

I'd always been a tomboy, but I'd never actually worn men's clothes before, and on top of that I'd chopped off all my hair."

Katie interrupted Cassidy there. "And you didn't feel you should've given your folks the heads-up about any of that before showing up?"

"Nope. I just said, '*Hi, Mom and Dad, I'd like you to meet my girlfriend, Jen.*'"

"So what did your parents do?"

"My mother took me aside and said, '*So was this your way of coming out to us?*' Then she softened and said, '*Jen seems like a very nice girl.*'

"I said, '*She is.*'

"She said, '*And very pretty.*'

"I said, '*I know.*'

"Then she said, '*I just don't understand why you can't let yourself look more like her. She wears dresses and makeup.*'"

Cassidy looked straight into Katie's eyes then to read her expression, unsure if she'd absorbed her meaning. "So the gay thing was fine," Cassidy said. "It was my clothes she couldn't get past."

"Huh," Katie said. "That's interesting."

Cassidy reached for her wineglass. In her experience, when someone said something was interesting, it meant she'd somehow freaked them the hell out.

"Something tells me your path to adulthood went a little smoother than mine," Cassidy said, eager to change the subject. "Maybe because I saw all those old photos of you on your fridge. Your family looks . . ."

Katie fiddled with her cloth napkin. Had it been paper it may have been torn to shreds. "Let's just say our Thanksgivings are all about turkey, stuffing, and football."

"Women cooking in the kitchen," Cassidy said. "Boys on the couch watching TV."

Katie's face shot up. "Excuse me?"

"I'm not passing judgment—"

"It sure sounds like you are."

"I'm sorry." Cassidy tried to backpedal. "You're right. Maybe that's not at all how it was at your house."

Katie cracked a smile. "Actually, that's exactly what it's like in my house, but that still doesn't give you the right to be uppity about it."

"It doesn't drive you nuts, though?" Cassidy said. "That double standard?"

"So what you're saying is"—Katie leaned in and rested her hand on top of Cassidy's—"you're the way you are because you hate doing dishes?"

Cassidy had to laugh. "You might be on to something."

Their plates were cleared, the disaster remnants of their feast cleaned away. In the heat of discussion, one of them had blown out their table's candle, but Cassidy hadn't noticed until their waitress relit it. The wall of quotations behind Katie flickered like a nervous poem.

Katie may have been the most traditional girl that Cassidy had ever sat down to a meal with. She radiated obedience, but instead of finding this off-putting, it only drew in Cassidy more. How rare to encounter someone so classic and authentic—so timeless.

"I enjoyed college, had lots of friends." Katie swirled her wine. "Not like now. I got lazy about friendships after Paul Michael. His friends became mine, and now I'm paying for it. I lost my entire friend group in one fell swoop."

Cassidy was already calculating ways to prolong the life of their meal when their waitress set down a giant piece of molten chocolate cake and two forks.

Hallelujah, Cassidy thought, even as she pushed the plate closer to Katie. "I'm not really one for desserts."

"Neither am I," Katie said. "But one bite couldn't hurt. We wouldn't want to anger Raquel."

She handed Cassidy one of the forks and dug into the cake with the other. "God, that is good."

Cassidy surrendered, forked herself a bite, and then said with as much levity as she could muster, "Since you don't have any other friends to meet up with tonight, why don't you come out to the Scene after this? That's where I'm headed."

"Tempting," Katie said. "But I think I'll pass."

"But you're tempted."

"I'm more tired than tempted," Katie said.

"I'll order us some espresso."

Katie smiled politely, and Cassidy understood she was pushing too hard.

"I should head home." Katie reached for her bag. "Can we get the check?"

"No," Cassidy said. "It's on me. It'll only come to like five dollars, so don't worry about it. But I am going to go pop into the kitchen to say thanks."

Katie stood up. "This was fun. We should do it again."

Cassidy reached for her suit jacket from the back of her chair. "Yeah? You're not just teasing me?"

"I might be," Katie said.

Cassidy tried not to linger on the hint of flirtation in those final words as she watched Katie walk out of the restaurant. Instead, she tossed a breath mint into her mouth and made her way to the kitchen.

Raquel was in the middle of scolding a line cook for dicing an onion that should have been minced. When she noticed Cassidy, she came right over. "I see you're back into straight girls," she said. "Is this one married like the last one?"

Cassidy took the hit. "I just came to say thanks for the fine treatment."

"I should have warned that poor girl." Raquel moved in closer than she needed to be.

Cassidy could smell the sweat and stock on her skin, and it made her hungry all over again. "It's not like that," Cassidy said. "She's just a friend from work."

"Mmm-hmm," Raquel said. She still hadn't moved away.

Cassidy could feel the sous-chef and line cooks looking on.

"What time are you getting out of here tonight?" Cassidy asked.

"You wish." Raquel shook her head and returned to the faulty onions.

Cassidy left a stack of twenties on the counter before making her exit.

SEVEN

Katie decided to walk the twenty minutes home. Buzzed and energized and full of chocolate and mercury, part of her wished she had gone with Cassidy to whatever hellhole she was off to, just so she could keep moving.

Cassidy could come on strong, that was for sure, but Katie found Cassidy's self-assuredness and even her occasional obnoxiousness intriguing. She seemed to really know how to live, to always know what she wanted. Katie could have learned a thing or two from the way Cassidy conducted herself.

Katie thought back to her first date with Paul Michael, when he took her to the opera—the real opera, the one Katie had grown up seeing in movies and on television. Before the show, Paul Michael ordered them French wine at the concession stand using the correct pronunciation, and it dawned on her all at once just how much she could learn from this man. "Thank you," she remembered saying, conscious to not draw out the *yooouuu*, when Paul Michael handed her that twenty-dollar glass of opera wine.

Katie walked along West Fourth Street. The night was cool and moonlit. Rowdy groups of twentysomethings, not so much younger than her, ran circles around her tense business suit. NYU kids most likely, fresh on a new school year. Along Washington Square Park, she passed a group of young men drumming on buckets. She wanted to join them, to bang on something, too. She wanted to dance.

Would she ever hang out with Cassidy again? Maybe. Probably, in fact. Why the heck not? Cassidy apparently had an in at every female-run restaurant in town.

Entering her lonely apartment killed some but not all of Katie's exhilaration. She was still restless as she changed into a T-shirt and sweat pants, and fidgety as she flipped through TV channels. She settled on a crime show where some girl had gone and gotten herself kidnapped and now a bunch of men had to find her—but she couldn't focus on it.

Katie felt strange, first on her walk home, and now here again, like her bodily senses had all been shaken awake and she couldn't get them back to sleep. It was possible she was nervous, but what about? She tried lying down, then sat back up, shifted her legs. There wasn't really any question that what she felt was aroused. Nothing about this procedural drama she was watching was the least bit stimulating, and yet somewhere within her there was a heat, a throbbing that would not quit.

She really needed to get out more if this was what happened when she went someplace new, had a little fun.

Katie brought her computer onto her lap. She would go on a date, a real date, even though she barely knew how because she'd hardly ever done it. Everything Katie knew about adult dating she'd learned from that home wrecker, Amy. Still, it would be enough to get by.

Katie was well versed in the various apps, but from witnessing Amy's constant swiping left and right, the idea of subjecting herself to that made Katie's stomach ache. An old-fashioned website seemed more appropriate if a proper date was what she was after, and she remembered the importance of choosing a site that charged a fee in order to filter out the riffraff.

She located one, and the online form seemed easy enough to work through.

I am a WOMAN seeking a MAN between ages: 25 and 35

Hold on. Best to be as specific as possible. She changed it to "between ages: 28 and 33."

Near zip code: 10014

Your height: 5'9"

Your hair color: blond

Your eye color: blue

Your body type: athletic

Your best feature: . . .

Do you smoke? No.

How often do you drink? Umm, lately?

About me and what I'm looking for . . .

Katie thought hard about this one. What did she honestly want? This was her chance to get it right.

I want to get over my ex, she wrote. And then deleted it.

I want to fall in love, she wrote instead, and then deleted that.

She just didn't know.

How could she not know?

About me and what I'm looking for . . .

Katie wrote: *I want to have some fun.*

That seemed vague enough to get somebody's attention, didn't it?

⋰♡⋱

Katie had not imagined that she would wake up to an inbox full of winks and messages and offers of intercourse, but this was exactly the case as she sat at her kitchen table with a cup of coffee and scrolled through her many virtual suitors. It was a mixed bag. From Paulie in Bay Ridge, who expressed interest in fucking her so hard, to Mike in Crown Heights, who expressed interest in fucking her so hard, to David in midtown, who expressed interest in fucking her so hard. At this rate she would have to grow another few holes just to keep up with it all. So much for the site's paywall working as a filter against losers.

Then Katie struck upon Jeremy in Chelsea, a good-looking, brown-haired, brown-eyed, six-foot-tall finance professional who enjoyed cycling, playing basketball, and going to nice restaurants. He did not express explicit interest in fucking Katie so hard but implied that he wouldn't be opposed to doing so. He complimented her photos and asked her out straightaway. The tone of his message was measured but confident and not a direct threat to any of her body parts, so she messaged him back something equally measured and confident with a little flirtation added in for good measure.

Just when Katie arrived at her office, she got a message back from him. *Are you free Saturday night by any chance?*

She wrote back: *By chance I am.*

Great. I'll make a reservation for 8 pm. Sound good?

Katie didn't really know how to do this online dating thing, but she got the immediate impression that there wasn't much conversation involved, so all she wrote back was: *Great.* Then she tried to calculate how much time she had to get herself up to snuff. Maybe a new dress, a mani/pedi, a wax. Not necessarily in that order. The wax probably needed to be prioritized.

Of course Katie couldn't get appointments at any of her regular places for these services because she chose to live in a city where you had to buy movie tickets a week in advance, so the next evening after work, she found herself at a random corner "spa" that was probably a money-laundering front. An angry-faced stranger was shredding her nether regions when her cell phone pinged.

Katie froze at the sight of Cassidy's name. *Had fun at dinner,* she'd written. *Lemme know if you're around this weekend.*

"Ow!"

"Sorry," Katie's angry-faced torturer said, but she did not seem very sincere.

Katie ignored Cassidy's text and switched her phone to silent.

By the time she left her apartment to meet up with Jeremy, Katie was bare and smooth and feeling confident in her new cobalt-blue wrap dress that made her eyes pop like she'd Insta-filtered herself with X-Pro II.

Jeremy was waiting outside the restaurant for her when she arrived, which she thought very gentlemanly. He recognized her right away and went in for a peck on the cheek.

So far so good. Katie had been concerned Jeremy might look older, balder, shorter, and overall less attractive than he did in his photos, but for the most part his full head of brown hair appeared the same as it did in that photo of him on his mountain bike, and he seemed to be a legitimate six feet tall. She checked out his shoes. They were brown leather derbys, clean and unscuffed, appropriate with his dark navy jeans and dress shirt. Not bad, she thought. Not bad at all.

He'd chosen Salinas, an ideal date restaurant thanks to its sexy atmosphere and flattering lighting. They were seated in the back garden, which had a retractable glass roof and a stone fireplace. They ordered wine and tapas and got to talking about themselves.

Katie couldn't find anything seriously wrong with this guy. He did brag about himself a little too much, but mostly he was doing his best to impress her and not stare too much at her plunging neckline. Overall Jeremy was a catch, and yet as dinner proceeded, Katie couldn't help but notice that she was kind of bored while he went on about his recent trip to Rwanda.

"It isn't for everyone," he said. "Hiking through rain forest, scaling mountains with slopes you wouldn't believe. But to have the opportunity to look directly into the eyes of a mountain gorilla and to see how expressive they are. It made me question what it even means to be human."

It was all Katie could do to not fall asleep into her *arroz de pato*. To Jeremy's credit, he caught on that anthropomorphism was not the most efficient route to her heart, so he quickly transitioned to his job. How hard he worked. How much responsibility he had. How many millions of dollars of other people's money he was responsible for. Standard investment banker banter.

"So what kind of law do you practice?" he asked her finally.

"I'm at Dorchester Nevins Dunn," Katie said. "In structured finance."

Jeremy recalculated something in his mind and then smiled. "So does this mean you're gonna bill me by the hour for this date?"

Katie forced a laugh because he was trying. It wasn't his fault that this felt like a job interview—she was just out of practice.

She could tell by the flush to his face that he liked her. And once he learned that Katie wasn't some public defender with big dreams or wide-eyed counsel to a nonprofit, he seemed to recognize that she wasn't so fragile, that he didn't have to be too careful with her and his best behavior could go right out the window with his sensitive guy's Rwandan gorilla trek. He flipped on the switch to his alpha male.

Their waiter presented them with the *postres* menu, and Jeremy didn't bother looking at his. "My apartment is really close to here," he said. "Just two blocks away."

Katie looked up from her menu. "Is it?"

Smooth, she thought. Real smooth.

"Want to skip *postres*?" he asked.

Was that any way to ask a lady to go to bed with you? But then again, why not? She was trying to try new things. That's what this whole night was about.

Just like that they were in Jeremy's living room making out like animals, animals with zero to offer on what it meant to be human, animals that were eating each other's faces. He unbuttoned his clean-cut dress shirt, and Katie was pleasantly taken aback by the Clark Kent surprise of his cut chest and abs.

"Do you have a condom?" she asked.

He nodded, scrambled to his nightstand, and they moved to his bed.

This was what she wanted, she told herself as Jeremy slid off her dress. This was what she came here for.

He climbed on top of her, and she closed her eyes.

This man was a stranger. This stranger was about to be inside her.

"Stop. I'm sorry." She shoved Jeremy off her.

He sat up, sweating, breathing hard. "What's the matter?"

"I'm sorry. This isn't me." She sprang up from the bed and scrambled for her shoes.

"Wait. You're leaving? Did I do something wrong?"

"Not at all." She wiggled her dress back on. "This was all my fault."

He moved to get up, wrapping the sheets around his waist.

"No, stay," Katie said, extending her arm as if to shield herself. "I'll let myself out."

She couldn't get away from Jeremy fast enough. Out on the street, she power-walked down Ninth Avenue like she'd just escaped a burning building that she herself had set on fire.

Her mind started spinning, and before she could stop it from happening, she became a girl in a slutty dress marching down the street while crying. She had to sit down on a cement slab in front of an abandoned construction site to catch her breath.

What the hell was happening to her? Something felt seriously and perhaps medically wrong. She needed to call someone, a friend. She took out her phone and started scrolling, but there was no one. She was having a nervous breakdown, hyperventilating, and there was no one!

The only recent activity on her phone was that text from Cassidy, which she'd never responded to. She wished she hadn't ignored it now that going home alone might result in a 911 call and an ambulance ride to Bellevue. Did Bellevue still exist? It was possible that even a famed mental hospital would fail her in her hour of need.

She started to text Cassidy: *I need help.* But she'd only typed *I need* when she accidently hit *send*, forcing her to compose a second text of only *Help*, which appeared even more pathetic and alarming as a stand-alone word. Which meant she had to send a third text to try to sound less nuts. *I can't go home. Are you out?*

Cassidy, bless her heart, wrote back right away. *Where are you?*

Katie began to write, *Construction site,* but thought it better to just give her cross streets.

Her phone suddenly rang, and she got so startled she nearly dropped it into a pile of rusted scaffolding pipe. "Hello?"

Cassidy's voice was on the other end of the line. "Katie, what's going on?"

"Oh nothing, I just . . ."

"You don't sound so good," she said, and that was probably because Katie had started to cry again. "Did something happen?" Cassidy asked.

"I don't know, I was at dinner and then this guy's apartment, and now I'm on the street, Ninth Avenue, I think, in Chelsea."

"Listen," Cassidy said. "You're five minutes from my apartment. I'll text you the address, okay? The doorman will let you up. I'll be there in fifteen minutes, tops."

"Will you really?" Katie choked the words out through her sobby throat.

"I'll meet you there in fifteen," Cassidy said. "I promise."

"Will they seriously let me in without you there?"

"Yeah, just ask for Brandon if you have a problem."

They hung up, and Cassidy's text came through with her address.

It was possible that Katie's nervous breakdown was simply a panic attack, because she felt calmer already, just knowing that she had someplace to go and someone to talk to.

In a few short blocks her breathing returned to normal and she was in front of Cassidy's building and holy shit, was this really where Cassidy lived? It was that crazy blue-glass building on West Eighteenth that curved like a curtain blowing in the wind. Katie entered like she wasn't a madwoman who'd just cried off all her eye makeup and approached the concierge.

"Excuse me," she said. "Are you Brandon?"

"I'm Frank. Brandon's not here, but how can I help you?"

"I'm a friend of Cassidy Price's. She'll be here in a few minutes, but she told me to ask to be let up to her apartment."

He nodded like this was a regular thing, took a quick look at Katie's driver's license, and then went to get a key from somewhere.

Frank accompanied Katie to the elevator and up the many floors to Cassidy's apartment. "Here we are," he said, unlocking her door, swinging it open, and clicking on the lights. "Can I help you with anything else?"

Whoa. This was the most beautiful and gigantic apartment Katie had ever seen. Paul Michael would have soiled himself over the design of the place.

"No, I'm good, thanks," she said, walking across the vast living room floor in a half-hypnotized state.

Frank left, closing the door behind him, and Katie did a 180 to take it all in, the panoramic views of Manhattan, the Hudson River, and the High Line. There was a certain masculinity to the place, in the way it was decorated. Lots of sleek black and rich browns in the living room, stainless steel and walnut wood in the kitchen. If she didn't know better, she would have guessed this place belonged to a man who was single, and possibly Bruce Wayne.

The bathroom was even more spectacular than she was anticipating—marble countertops, a limestone floor, a glassed-in shower with one of those crazy showerheads that rained down on you like actual rain. She couldn't help but notice Cassidy's products around the sink—hair tonics and creams in dark bottles and circular metal tins. Moisturizers and lotions with foreign labels. Not a pink razor to be found. No lipstick tubes or blush brushes.

Katie knew it was wrong, but she had to inspect the bedroom. This was like being left unattended on the best HGTV episode of all time—how could she not check out the bedroom?

Like the rest of the place it was sparsely but impeccably decorated, immaculate to the point of being almost scary. The centerpiece was a walk-in closet that would have made Carrie Bradshaw swoon, except that it was filled with only dark suits, crisp dress shirts, and men's shoes. Where did Cassidy keep her nonwork clothes? Katie opened the top drawer of her dresser and—eek. Men's briefs? She slammed the drawer shut and suddenly felt sick.

She rushed back to the living room.

Maybe she should go. Maybe this was a mistake.

Just then, she heard a key in the door. She sat down on the leather sofa as Cassidy stepped inside.

EIGHT

It was only around eleven p.m., but Cassidy was lit. She couldn't recall the name of the girl she was sucking face with up against the bathroom wall at Metropolis—Laila, was it? Or Laina, or Lainey. What did it matter? She tugged at Cassidy's belt buckle as they stumbled into the doorless stall designated for this exact purpose. The important part was that Cassidy was feeling no pain. She remembered nothing of her day, her week, her life. If the girl's name was collateral damage, so be it. Cassidy went at her neck, unbuttoned her blouse. Everything was vibrating.

No, not everything, Cassidy realized. It was her pocket. The vibration was coming from her phone, not her insides.

Cassidy hadn't been thinking about Katie. She had very specifically not been thinking about Katie since she'd texted her to say she'd enjoyed their dinner and got no reply—but still she had to take out her phone and look.

There was Katie's name staring back at her.

I need, Katie had written. "Whoa, whoa. Hang on a sec," Cassidy said to Laila or Laina or Lainey.

"Are you seriously texting someone right now?" The girl's bright yellow blouse was wide open, exposing a skimpy bra the color of ripe watermelon.

"I'm so sorry." Cassidy zipped up her pants and rebuckled her belt. "I have to make a quick call."

Cassidy bumbled out of the bathroom with her phone to her ear as it dialed Katie's number. It was already ringing by the time she made it outside to the sidewalk.

"Hello? Katie?" Cassidy yelled into her phone, covering her free ear with the palm of her hand, but she still couldn't hear over the street traffic. "Are you crying?"

Katie was somewhere in Chelsea, that much she understood.

"You're right near my apartment," Cassidy shouted. She held out her arm to hail a cab, or rather her arm flew into the air all on its own, frantic and determined. Desperate, really.

A cab pulled up just as whatever her name was burst through Metropolis's door. "You're leaving?" Her yellow blouse was neatly rebuttoned, but the rest of her was chaotic. "You were just going to leave me like that?"

Cassidy hurried into the cab and slammed the door shut. "Emergency!" she yelled through the open window. "I'm having an emergency."

꙳♡꙳

Cassidy did her best to sober up on the twelve-minute cab ride home by taking deep breaths and chewing on breath mints. She wasn't sure what she was walking into, if some tragedy had occurred, but whatever it was, Katie had thought to call her—and that had to mean something. When Katie had ignored her text, a siren had gone off in Cassidy's ears, a terrorizing sound of alarm that would not stop.

It went quiet at the sight of Katie seated on her living room sofa.

Katie was slouched over with her deep-blue dress hanging half off her shoulder. Her eye makeup was smudged, and her hair was tied up in a messy ponytail.

"What's going on?" Cassidy crossed the room with apprehension. "Are you okay?"

Katie looked at the floor, so Cassidy brought her voice down to a gentle tone, the kind you might use with a child you're trying not to frighten. "Did something happen?"

"Not like you're thinking," Katie said. "I'm just having a hard time."

"Oh good. I mean, that's understandable, that you're having a hard time." Cassidy stumbled over her relief that Katie wasn't in real crisis, uncertain now of how to proceed. "Can I fix you a drink? I've got a bottle of Evan Williams."

"You do not," Katie said. "Did you know they make that right near where I grew up?"

Of course Cassidy did. She'd special-ordered the bottle and had it overnighted, not because she imagined Katie would ever be present to share it but because she'd had an unrelenting craving for Kentucky bourbon since they first met.

Cassidy half-filled two rocks glasses, then sat at a safe distance from Katie, in her leather lounge chair. She would not allow herself to drink another sip of alcohol, but she had to fix herself a glass for appearance's sake.

Katie sipped her bourbon, cupping the glass as if it held warm tea. "This is delicious."

"Good," Cassidy said.

Tears started running down Katie's face again, maybe from the simple kindness Cassidy was offering, maybe from the taste of home. "I'm sorry," she said. "I don't even know what's happening to me. My emotions are all over the place."

"It's okay." Cassidy leaned forward on her chair. "You don't have to apologize."

"I don't even know why I called you."

"That's okay, too."

The tears continued, and Cassidy could see that Katie was desperate for something. Comfort? Human contact? Anything to feel better.

Cassidy watched her cry for longer than she could bear

before setting her bourbon on the table, rising from her chair, and joining Katie on the couch.

Katie inched closer to her the moment she sat down. "What were you doing when I called you?" she asked.

"Nothing much."

"I hope I didn't ruin your night."

"You didn't."

Katie rested her head on Cassidy's shoulder. "Are you sure?"

Cassidy heard herself exhale, like a release valve had been pulled. "Positive." She placed her hand on Katie's back. It was a consolation touch, no different from any friend comforting another in an hour of need. "I'm glad you're here."

Katie lifted her head from Cassidy's shoulder, looked her right in the eyes. "I am, too."

Cassidy didn't entirely trust herself to not pull Katie in closer. She'd ingested far too much alcohol to judge for certain what was happening in this moment, if the spark she felt between them was real or not.

"I think you should stay here tonight," Cassidy said, before Katie could say anything else. "In my guest room. You can hang out, do your thing, but I'm going to go to bed now. Okay?"

Katie's expression changed in a way that Cassidy couldn't read. For a second she thought Katie might start crying again, or lean in to kiss her, or both.

"I don't—" Katie said, and then stopped. "Okay."

"Great." Cassidy launched off the couch in the direction of the guest room, which no one but Gina had ever slept in— girls who spent the night usually did so in Cassidy's bed.

She detoured into the bathroom, flipped on the light, and waited for Katie to catch up to her. "There are towels there if you want to take a shower. New toothbrushes here." She opened a drawer below the sink.

Katie peered into the drawer. "Why do you have so many?"

Cassidy searched her hazy brain for a second. "I like to replace them fairly often," she said. "Easiest to buy in bulk."

A lie. They were one-night-stand toothbrushes, of course.

Cassidy continued on into the guest room. "The cleaning service just came yesterday, so the sheets on the bed are fresh." She untucked the bedspread to reveal the freshly laundered sheets.

Katie grazed her hand across their surface. "Soft."

"They're Italian," Cassidy said. "A thousand twenty thread count."

"Who knows their sheets' thread count?" Katie said. "I guess you're as into textiles as you are toothbrushes."

"Pajamas." Cassidy snapped her fingers. "You'll need pajamas. Be right back." She jogged into her bedroom, realizing that she was sweating gin. She could smell it on herself as she dug through her dresser drawers. She returned to the guest room with her only pair of sweat pants neatly folded on top of a white T-shirt.

Katie was sitting on the edge of the bed. "Those look normal enough," she said.

Cassidy handed her the clothes. "What were you expecting?"

"I don't know. Some silk getup Hugh Hefner might wear?"

"Good night, Katie."

"Hold on." Katie held up the sweat pants. "Are these cashmere?"

Cassidy nodded.

"Who buys cashmere sweat pants?"

"Good night, Katie," Cassidy said again, this time making her escape and closing the door behind her.

Cassidy couldn't sleep, not with Katie in the next room just a few feet away, so she did what she always did when she needed to burn off some energy in the middle of the night—crunches, followed by push-ups, followed by crunches, followed by push-ups, until there was nothing left in the tank.

The repetition soothed her, and the pain would eventually be strong enough to force out every last thought, like whether Katie was awake, if she was twisting and turning and wondering what would have happened if Cassidy hadn't retreated.

Twenty-one, twenty-two, twenty-three . . .

Would anything have happened?

Twenty-four, twenty-five, twenty-six . . .

It couldn't all be in Cassidy's head that they had a connection, but she'd done the right thing, putting a stop to it. The wrong thing would have been to take advantage of Katie. To be led by her own desire when she knew the girl was a mess and in a total tailspin. The best Cassidy could do was duck out of the way.

Thirty.

Cassidy sprang up with one knee and planted her hands firmly on the floor beneath her shoulders. She lowered her body down, careful to keep her back flat.

One, two, three . . .

Then again, wasn't Cassidy also being taken advantage of? It was Katie who probably wanted to use her as an experiment, as a distraction, as a painkiller.

Since when did Cassidy not want to be used?

She lived for the agony of doomed erotic collision, for self-sabotage, for *I know this is going to hurt but I'm going to do it anyway, in fact that's why I'm going to do it.*

Cassidy's phone dinged with a text, and she jumped to standing. What if it was Katie from the next room, asking for company, asking for more?

She tugged the hem of her boxer briefs down from where they'd ridden up on her thighs, then reached for the phone.

It was a text from Gina: *Heard you booked it out of the met like a maniac. WTF?*

Christ. WTF was right.

Another text: *Who wuz the girl?*

Cassidy sat on the edge of her bed and wrote back: *Which girl?*

You're sleeping with her. I know you are.

Who?

You know who.

I wish, Cassidy wrote, and then deleted it. *I'm not,* Cassidy wrote instead. *But she's sleeping in my guest room.*

Gina wrote: *She's staying over and you're not gonna sleep with her? This is worse than I thought.*

Cassidy chucked her phone aside. This was worse than she'd thought, too, which was why she had to keep her guard up. She had to protect herself. She needed to stay the hell away from Katie. Do the opposite of what her impulses told her to do.

She dropped back down into a plank.

Not only for Katie's good. But for her own.

One, two, three . . .

For once she would do the right thing.

NINE

Katie woke up and yawned her way into Cassidy's kitchen, following the scent of fresh coffee. There she found Cassidy wide awake in jogging shorts and a sweat-wicking tank top. Katie was startled by the sight of so much bare skin— Cassidy's calves, thighs, and shoulders.

"Wow," Katie said. "You are really fit."

"You're up early." Cassidy appeared surprised to see her, like she'd either forgotten Katie had spent the night or was trying to sneak out unnoticed. "I was about to go for a run," she said. "There's coffee for you."

Katie poured herself a cup. Something about the way Cassidy was looking at her, or refusing to look at her, brought a knot to her stomach. There had been a moment of weirdness last night. Katie hadn't been sure of it at first, but Cassidy's avoidance of her now confirmed it.

Though it was possible Cassidy was just too embarrassed for Katie to look at her. If she were Cassidy, she might have a hard time looking at her, too. What had she been thinking, calling this almost stranger in tears—and then spending the night in her spare room and her pajamas?

"Hang out as long as you like," Cassidy said, while stretching her quads. She may as well have put up a wall between them.

"Can I come with you?" Katie asked.

She'd surprised herself by asking. A final apology and walking her embarrassment home would have been much more appropriate, but the idea of dashing through sunlight and fresh air—not alone with her sadness, but with a friend—was too enticing to pass up. Its appeal trumped Katie's shame.

Cassidy clasped an exercise watch to her wrist. "Do you run?"

"Yeah I run," Katie said.

Cassidy appeared dubious. "I usually do seven miles on the weekends."

Katie chugged some coffee, then set down the mug. "Let's make it eight."

"I'm not one to decline a challenge," Cassidy said. "But

you don't have any sneakers. And, no offense, but I've seen you try to run in high heels before."

"I'm a size ten," Katie said. "Do you have a pair I can borrow?"

Cassidy closed one eye, no less dubious. "I wear a ten."

"That makes sense." Katie gestured toward Cassidy's body. "We're kind of the same size. You're just . . ."

"Careful," Cassidy said.

"What? I was going to say you're more muscular. And I have more . . ." Katie drifted off, understanding now about being careful. "I am going to need a sports bra. Can I wear one of . . . yours?"

"Right, okay." Cassidy averted her eyes and moved toward her bedroom. "It'll probably be too small."

Katie almost followed Cassidy into the bedroom, but she stayed put, sensing she was not welcome there. "That's okay," she said, trying to sound nonchalant. "I like to keep 'em nice and cozy when I run."

Cassidy was silent. All Katie could hear was the opening and closing of drawers. She was tempted to ask if it would be weird for Cassidy to have Katie wearing her bra, or if it was weird for Cassidy to wear a bra at all. It was kind of weird for Katie to imagine Cassidy wearing a bra, or anything so female beneath her clothes. Did she keep her bras in the same drawer with her men's underwear?

Cassidy returned from the bedroom with a pair of sneakers, shorts, socks, and a T-shirt. A sports bra was hidden somewhere in the middle of the pile.

Katie went to the guest room to change, noticing this black pair of shorts and charcoal shirt were definitely not from the Nike women's department, where almost every article was splashed with hot pink or baby blue and the shorts lacked this under-layer that she assumed was for genitalia holding. But the clothes fit Katie fine; they were just a little less formfitting than she was accustomed to.

She returned to the living room dressed and ready to go.

"Looking good," Cassidy said.

Katie smiled. "I feel like I look like you."

"Not quite."

Outside, the morning was crisp and bright. They jogged west to Chelsea Piers, then south along the Hudson all the way to Battery Park, talking about waterfront real estate and climate change and the preposterousness of waterfront real estate prices in spite of rising sea levels. On their way north again, they addressed the faults of the federal government's legislative branch. Katie also learned that Cassidy had an aversion to raw carrots and anything lavender scented. And Katie shared with Cassidy how she despised goat cheese and loved pickles, and sometimes she went to the dog park even though she didn't own a dog.

There was a strange comfort that came from talking while not facing each other. Katie could look out over the water at the Statue of Liberty, or focus on not colliding with other runners or getting run over by a tourist on a Citi Bike, while telling stories about herself she might not have told otherwise.

What they didn't talk about was the moment of weirdness, and the more Katie thought about it, the more she wanted to talk about it—the more she wished Cassidy would be willing to talk about it. But each time Katie made a feeble attempt to bring it up, Cassidy redirected their conversation.

When Katie said, "I know I seemed totally out of it last night, but just so you know, I wasn't drunk or anything," Cassidy said, "It would have been okay if you were. How'd you like the Evan Williams? Good as back home?"

When Katie said, "I called you last night in such a state because I tried to go on a date with a guy I met online," Cassidy said, "Good for you for getting yourself back out there. Which dating sites do you use?"

Maybe it was better this way, just letting it go, chalking it up to confusion.

Cassidy was doing her a favor by refusing to let her overthink it.

Katie scanned the horizon, straightening her neck and back. Her shoulders, she noticed, were creeping up on her ears, and she was clenching her fists, so she dropped her arms to her sides and shook them out to release the tension.

"We're coming up on eight miles." Cassidy showed Katie her watch.

"Already?" Katie said. "I feel like I could keep going."

Cassidy seemed equally unwilling to rest, so they kept running, pushing themselves, delighting in the exertion. Eventually they stopped talking, but their legs continued on in sync, paced to one another.

With the sun on her face, endorphins coursing through her brain, Katie was reminded of the thrill she felt on her walk home from dinner with Cassidy, of the carelessness Cassidy embodied, the buzz of selfish freedom.

They finally stopped to walk after ten miles, when they found themselves back at Chelsea Piers. Spent and breathing hard, they bought some water from a pushcart, chugged it, and then threw themselves onto the grass blissfully exhausted.

The grass was cool and prickly on the backs of Katie's arms and legs. She could smell the rich dirt beneath it. "I can't remember the last time I lay on the ground like this," she said. "Without a sheet or blanket or anything."

Cassidy's eyes were closed, but Katie could see her chest rising and falling with her breath. "Me neither."

"Why is that?" Katie said. "It's wonderful."

Cassidy smiled, still with her eyes closed. "I don't know."

There was no good reason for Katie to remain at Cassidy's once her purse and keys and last night's dress were in hand, but when Cassidy asked her to stay for lunch, she agreed before she could think of a reason not to.

Katie was the first to shower. In Cassidy's spectacular bathroom, she turned on the showerhead and closed her eyes as a steamy waterfall rained over her shaky muscles. On a narrow shelf at eye level was a black razor that sat on a silver shaving stand. Alongside it was a small jar labeled *Crème à Raser*. Katie left the razor setup alone, but she lathered each aching limb with Cassidy's luxuriant anise-scented soap and cleansed the sweat from her hair with Cassidy's European shampoo, newly sentient of her living, breathing, thriving body.

There was that heat again, that throbbing that would not quit.

What would she do, she wondered, if Cassidy opened the bathroom door right then and slipped into the shower with her? How would her body react?

But what kind of thought was that to have?

Katie seemed to be all out of whack. She was reminded of the way some of the horses in the stables back home would act up at the change of season. Late fall would approach, and a usually calm and steady mare would start behaving like she'd been possessed, walking with a heightened awareness, overalert to every sight, sound, and smell. This was how Katie felt here in Cassidy's shower, wholly in the power of her bodily urges, spooked by an almost imperceptible change in the air.

Katie revved the faucet hard and to the right for a surge of icy cold, and then stepped out of the shower onto the slate tile floor one foot at a time.

She wrapped herself in Cassidy's soft terry-cloth robe. On her way to the living room, her dripping-wet hair left a trail of droplets behind her.

Cassidy was seated on the couch bent over her laptop, still in her exercise clothes. She looked up at Katie, then immediately back down.

Katie watched her and tried to name exactly what it was that she felt toward Cassidy in that moment. Affinity? Attraction? She was objectively attractive, gender aside. Striking even, and a charmer when she cared to be. If Cassidy were a man, Katie might have crawled onto the couch, let her robe fall open, and seen what happened.

But she wasn't a man.

"I'm ordering us some lunch." Cassidy turned her laptop around and shot up to standing. "Just pick out whatever you want and then hit *send*. I'm going to hop in the shower."

"Are you sure I'm not overstaying my welcome?" Katie asked, while blocking Cassidy's route to the bathroom.

Cassidy smiled at Katie's refusal to let her by. "I'm not even going to dignify that question with a response."

"I'll head home after lunch," Katie said.

"You don't have to." Cassidy remained still, no longer making any effort to pass. "I like having you here."

"Do you have big plans tonight?"

Cassidy took a half step backward. "I wouldn't call them big. There's a barbecue at Metropolis every Sunday. Tonight's the last one of the season."

"Is it fun?"

"Why do you ask?"

"I don't know," Katie said. "Maybe I'll come by."

Cassidy seemed to consider this. "You keep showing up at Metropolis, and people might get the wrong idea."

In spite of herself, Katie felt a thrill shoot up her spine. She shrugged her shoulders and stepped aside then, allowing Cassidy to make her way to the shower.

❤

Katie stood in front of her closet wearing nothing but her black lace bra and underwear, trying not to think too much about where she was headed and why. She wanted to go to the bar, so she was going to go to the bar. It was as simple as that. She preferred to focus on her outfit. A barbecue called for casual, but she didn't want to go so casual that her lace undergarments felt bullied or out of place.

Of course this was the moment her mother chose to call

her. She swore the woman had a sixth sense for whenever Katie was doing something she wouldn't approve of.

"Hey, Mama," Katie answered, in a tone of voice that she hoped in no way revealed that she was standing in her underwear preparing to go to a barbecue that would blow her mother's head right from her body.

"I told you I want you checking in more often, now that you're living alone again," her mother said, not bothering with a hello.

"Sorry . . . I've just been busy."

"Busy doing what is what I want to know."

It was a mixed blessing that her mother knew nothing of FaceTime or Skype. On one hand, it allowed Katie to continue getting dressed during her mother's inquisition, but on the other it might have helped with her mother's relentless inability to visualize Katie's New York life. If she could actually have seen that Katie was okay, she might have worried less.

Katie could see almost exactly what her mother was doing in that moment, even without the help of an app. She would be talking to Katie from the kitchen, the phone crooked between her ear and her shoulder, while she went about preparing Sunday dinner—chuck roast with potatoes and carrots, or roast pork with applesauce, or maybe chicken and corn bread. There'd be a skillet sizzling with buttered green beans or buttermilk-dipped okra. Her mother would be wearing a brightly colored cotton top—turquoise or magenta or a flower pattern—and comfortable pants, but also a full face of makeup, with her highlighted hair blown to perfection.

"Have you heard anything from the professor?" she asked.

By "*the professor*," her mother meant Paul Michael, who she understood worked in the arts, but long ago she'd decided that—in her words—"he didn't just talk; he professed things. Plus, he looked like a college professor with those thick eyeglasses of his."

"No," Katie said. "I haven't heard anything from him, and I don't expect to."

"You just need to find somebody better," her mother said. "Somebody more like us. To get you halfway straight."

Dear lord. If her mother only knew where Katie was headed after she hung up this phone.

"Are you in for the night?" her mother asked.

There was that sixth sense again.

Katie hated to lie. Her mother had always been difficult, but she'd also been Katie's main confidant all her life. Katie had "ripped my guts out" (again, her mother's words) by moving to New York, and then made a bad situation worse by bringing home an "airy-fairy" boy like Paul Michael, and still her mother had not given up on her.

But telling her mother the truth this time, that she was off to a gay barbecue to meet up with her new gay best friend, was more than Minnie Daniels could reasonably bear. It would raise too many questions in her hidebound, alarmist mind. *What could you possibly have in common? Is she fixin' to get you to hate men? How do you expect to meet a good man if that's where you're whittling away your time?*

Katie considered it an act of love to reply, "Yeah, I'm in for the night."

"Are you eating?"

"I will have dinner." Katie filed through her closet hangers. "Yes."

"I wish you'd come home."

"I know, Mama, but I've got to go to work tomorrow."

Katie picked out possible skirt contenders while her mother persisted. "I haven't gotten a letter from you in ages."

"I'll write you one, I promise, but you have to let me off the phone first."

"My green beans are starting to burn up anyway."

"Okay then," Katie said, gladly accepting her mother's passive aggression with a *goodbye* and an *I love you* before ending the call.

Back to focusing on her outfit. Katie settled on a printed skirt and black moto jacket, then dug through her jewelry box, certain she had some accessory that could be read as Metropolis appropriate.

Aha. The fishhook-clasp leather wrap bracelet that she'd bought a year ago but never wore because Paul Michael said it looked "sadomasochistic in a Mapplethorpian kind of way." Perfect.

:♡:

When Katie arrived at the Met, Gina was leaning against the building, smoking a cigarette. She exhaled a gray cloud and whistled, which Katie interpreted as validation of her ensemble. Then Gina asked, "What in hell are you doing here?"

Inside, the bar was astonishingly uncrowded, and somehow this was worse than when it was full. Seeing Metropolis empty in the daylight was like looking at Darth Vader with his mask off—stripped of its prowess and capacity to intimidate, and all-around forlorn. But there was a raw vulnerability to it, too, that Katie found endearing. This larger-than-life space was in fact just a room like any other. It struck Katie then how much it was about the people who filled a space with drama and personality, with love and grudges and outsize emotion, that made a place what it was.

"Keep going." Gina followed behind Katie. "Everyone's in the back garden."

Katie continued on to the "back garden," which was actually just a concrete patio surrounded by a high wooden fence. A latticed veranda paradise this was not. And yet, the moment Katie stepped foot on that cracked concrete, she felt at home among the checkered tablecloths, the red and blue plastic cups, and the smell of singed meat.

"This way." Gina escorted Katie past two women in skinny white tank tops manning the grill, their nipples visible through the thin cotton.

Dahlia the bartender was pouring a pitcher of beer, wearing pigtails and a hot-pink bikini.

"How'd you get back in here?" she called out to Katie. "Didn't I put you on the Banned for Life list?"

Katie halted, and Dahlia's face broke into a warm smile. "I'm just playing with you, Wild Turkey. Welcome back. Make yourself at home."

Katie returned Dahlia's smile and relaxed just enough then to fully absorb the backyard-family-barbecue vibe of her surroundings. It occurred to her how long it had been since she'd gotten to kick back and enjoy a shitty hot dog and some cheap beer surrounded by friends. She suddenly wanted to pull her American flag bikini top out of retirement—the one Paul Michael forbade her from wearing in public—throw on some shorty-short Daisy Dukes, and get loud. Maybe try to talk everyone into a touch football game.

She and Gina reached a long rectangular table in the back that was already littered with potato-salad-splattered paper plates and half-eaten tofu pups. Seated at the table were Chef Becky and a few people Katie had been introduced to her last time at the Met—and there was Cassidy next to a girl Katie didn't recognize.

"Look who I found," Gina announced to the group.

Cassidy turned around, shocked to see Katie standing there, and not in a good way. She was a deer in headlights—no, she was a deer just downed by a Remington .308.

Hadn't Katie hinted hard enough that she might show up? Did Cassidy think she was bluffing?

Chef Becky leapt from her seat. "You came back to us! Come, come, sit down. I just got a fresh pitcher."

Katie approached Cassidy and stood oddly at the table's edge over the stranger who was seated between them.

"I didn't think you'd show," Cassidy said.

"Surprise," Katie said.

Everyone shifted one space over to make room for Katie at the table, so instead of getting to sit next to Cassidy, she was stuck beside this stranger.

"This is Annika," Cassidy said.

"Nice to meet you." Annika put out her hand.

Katie sized her up. She had long red hair, green eyes, and a scratchy voice like a sexy movie villain. She was pretty and stylish and capable of properly applying lipstick—which Katie was quickly beginning to realize was Cassidy's type.

"Annika's visiting from LA," Cassidy said. "She's working on a cooking show with Becky."

More lesbians in the food industry.

"Hey," Annika said. "Did you hear me?"

"I'm sorry," Katie said. "What?"

"Your bracelet." Annika touched the soft black leather encasing Katie's wrist. "I love it. I mean, it's basically a cock ring, but you wear it well." Then Annika let out this ba-ha-ha laugh that was unbelievably loud.

Cassidy laughed with her, and Katie noticed how Cassidy was hovering all close to Annika, and she was smiling wider than she normally did.

"So you're a food stylist." Cassidy reclaimed Annika's attention and direct eye contact. "Forgive my naiveté, but what does that mean exactly?"

"I dress up food," Annika said. "For photos and TV. You know the perfect cherry pies and turkey skin you see in magazines? That's all me. You'd be amazed by what I can do with a blowtorch and some PVA glue."

"I'm already amazed," Cassidy said.

Annika reached into her empty rocks glass, picked out an ice cube, and slipped it into her mouth. She asked Cassidy, "What do you do?"

"I'm a lawyer."

"Oh. That's . . ." Annika crunched hard on her ice.

"It's all right," Cassidy said. "You don't have to pretend it's cool."

"Okay, good," Annika said, a smidgeon too loud. "I won't. Ba-ha-ha-ha-ha!"

Katie claimed a plastic cup from the stack at the end of the table and poured herself some beer while Cassidy listened to Annika go on about LA: "It's so annoying how, like, no one talks about weed like it's a drug. They talk about it like it's a vegetable."

The beer was warm, but Katie drank it anyway.

"And you first met Becky on the set of *Knife Fight*?" Cassidy asked.

"Ugh! Yes. She tried to hit on me while cranking pork butts through a manual meat grinder. I was like, gross."

Katie poked at someone's abandoned paper plate with a plastic knife. She made a little hollow in a mound of potato salad and filled it with baked beans.

Annika was now going on about how to manipulate pancakes so the syrup glided perfectly over the edge: "First you stick cardboard between the layers, then you spray them with water-repellent Scotchgard. Then you feed 'em to your worst enemy. Ba-ha-ha-ha-ha!"

Over the course of the next hour, Annika's laugh got rowdier, her humor brassier, her voice sultrier.

Cassidy turned up her charm about as subtly as a dog coming into heat.

Katie couldn't decide which of them she wanted to smack across the face more. Cassidy, probably. Who was Annika to her? Nobody. While Cassidy was . . . well, whatever she was. Not a very nice friend at the moment, or very considerate.

Out of nowhere, a girl wearing overalls with only under-garments underneath came over to hit on Katie. She stood over her, leaning against the edge of the table, suggestively sucking on a lollipop. "Is this your first time here?" she asked between licks.

Katie watched Annika's hand travel to Cassidy's knee. Then she watched Annika lean in toward Cassidy's ear and whisper something. Katie couldn't make out exactly what, but she imagined it was something along the lines of "You are so goddamn sexy."

Cassidy glanced in Katie's direction for a split second be-fore turning right back to answer Annika. "So are you," she most likely said.

"Should we get out of here?" This part Annika announced loud enough for all to hear. "I'm staying at Becky's. It's just around the corner." She stood up before Cassidy could an-swer. "I'll get her keys."

Cassidy stood up, too, as Annika headed over to Chef Becky.

Katie reached for her purse. She wanted to do something to stop this. She couldn't let Cassidy go.

Becky, Katie noticed, looked to Cassidy once Annika got hold of her keys. In fact, it seemed to Katie like everyone was looking at Cassidy right then—but Cassidy was looking at her.

"You're leaving?" Katie asked, startled at finally having Cassidy's undivided attention. "With her?"

Cassidy nodded.

"Why?" Katie said.

Cassidy stood still, dumbfounded. "I don't know."

Katie stepped toward her. "I don't want you to."

"You don't?" Cassidy said.

"Hey, asshole," Annika called out from behind Cassidy with Becky's apartment keys in hand. "Get out of the way."

All drinking and laughter and chatter ceased.

Katie waited.

Time slowed down but also somehow sped up. Katie's senses heightened, her heart rate jumped, and she became conscious of every surrounding detail even as she fell into a hallucinatory, oblivious state that felt kaleidoscopically unreal.

Cassidy's kiss was hesitant at first, provisional, but soon they fell into a rhythm.

"What the fuck?" Annika's scratchy movie-villain voice pierced Katie's ears. "You New York bitches are all fucking crazy."

Others were whooping and howling.

"It's on!"

"I called it!"

"Everyone pay up!"

Cassidy was the first to pull away. "Leave with me," she said.

"Yes," Katie said. "Okay."

TEN

——————————

Cassidy rushed them out of the bar, to the street. The moment they climbed into a taxi she was ready to kiss Katie again, her mouth, her neck. All the questions disappeared; she could disregard holding back—Katie wanted this as much as she did, and this part Cassidy knew how to do.

"West Eighteenth and Tenth," she said to the driver, and leaned across the seat.

Katie was looking out the window. Cassidy admired her face in silhouette against the city passing by. She had the urge to reach over and sketch its outline on the glass.

By god, how she ached for this girl.

"Why were you being so god-awful mean to me?" Katie said, and only then did Cassidy realize that Katie was leaning on the door of the far side of the cab like she was considering jumping out.

"Wait. What?" Cassidy said.

"Why were you acting like that?" The hurt in Katie's voice was too familiar. "When I went there just to see you?"

But we were just making out, Cassidy wanted to say. *Can we just get back to doing that?*

Katie turned to look at her, finally, waiting for an answer Cassidy didn't have. Cassidy thought about bringing her mouth to Katie's again, to remind her that they'd already moved past this, that they were already moving forward.

Cassidy should say she was sorry. Why couldn't she just say that she was sorry?

Katie shook her head. "But watching you with that other girl," she said. "I got jealous. What do you think that means?"

Cassidy tried to maintain a neutral expression, to not startle Katie one way or the other. "I don't know."

"If you don't know," Katie said, "how am I supposed to know?"

Katie turned back to the window, and Cassidy let her do her ruminating in silence.

You got jealous because you like me, Cassidy thought, because you wanted me to take you home. Isn't that obvious?

When the taxi pulled up to the front of Cassidy's building, she stepped out onto the curb and held the door open for Katie, but Katie remained seated.

"I'm going to go home," Katie said.

Cassidy searched for the right words to put Katie at ease, to save the night, to convince her to come upstairs, but all she said was, "Okay."

Cassidy entered her apartment, looked around, and rubbed the back of her neck like she had whiplash. What the hell was she supposed to do now, after being ditched like that?

She considered turning around and going right back to the Met, but she didn't really feel like explaining how she ended up back there alone, especially to Annika. Or worse, Gina.

Instead she trudged into her kitchen, where she immediately noticed that Katie's coffee cup from that morning was still in the sink. She opened the fridge, stared into the light for a few seconds, and then closed it. She gazed into the fruit bowl on the counter, deliberating whether she felt like eating an apple, decided no, and then grabbed a lemon.

She would fix herself a proper drink, a Manhattan with a shaved lemon peel for garnish and all, and then she would find someone to come to her.

Why were you being so god-awful mean to me?

She slammed a glass onto her bar, threw in a perfect square of ice.

Why were you acting like that?

Bourbon. Vermouth. Bitters. Shake. Pour.

The lemon zest really did the trick. Pleased with herself, Cassidy carried the drink into the living room. She sat in her favorite Zanotta lounge chair and scrolled her phone.

Who was she in the mood for? She could have whomever she wanted. There were probably twenty girls in her phone whom she could text right now and have undressed within the hour. She specifically designed her life to function this way. She worked hard and played hard, and she didn't apologize. And anyway, she didn't tell Katie to show up at Metropolis; Katie did that all on her own.

She had nothing to feel bad about.

This was who she was. She had sex. It was basically her hobby. Why should she feel guilty about that all of a sudden?

Since her first college girlfriend this was how it had been. Cassidy had told Katie about Jen, but she'd failed to mention that what she and Jen did best was fuck, all the time. And that back then, Cassidy never imagined that she could be so carnal and uninhibited, or so fully satisfied by another person—so she surprised herself the first time she cheated on Jen with a girl from her Political Theory class. And the second time with a girl from the gym. And the third time with a girl who waited on her at Starbucks. But thinking of it now, Cassidy remembered how each indiscretion began as an innocent flirtation, a stroke of the ego that quickened over time until it progressed into something fated and unstoppable.

Maybe Cassidy didn't need to tell Katie any of that because Katie already knew. She sensed it in Cassidy's inability to convince her otherwise, and that's what sent her home. It was simple good intuition.

The way Katie looked at her in the cab—it was the same look that Jen had given her after she found her out, when on what would have been their six-month anniversary, Jen confronted Cassidy on the steps outside her dorm and asked, "What the fuck is wrong with you?"

What was wrong with her? A lot, most likely.

Cassidy sipped her Manhattan with one hand while furiously scrolling through names with the other. She reached the K's, and her phone's roll settled onto Katie's name like a losing slot machine.

The worst part was that she hadn't even gotten to sleep with Katie, and somehow she'd still managed to hurt her.

Why were you being so god-awful mean to me? Why were you acting like that?

Because she could. Because nothing got to her. Because this was what Cassidy did; she wrecked people.

ELEVEN

In her windowless office with glass walls, Katie tried to appear normal. Across the hall, she could see Marion, the perpetually bleary-eyed, prematurely graying senior associate with whom she was working on a new deal, pecking away at her computer while Katie pretended to be engaged with hers.

Beneath Katie's computer monitor, just to the right of her keyboard, sat her cell phone. She'd strategically barricaded it between two stacks of file folders, where it was safe from Marion's line of vision, or anyone else's who stepped inside.

The phone had not lit up all day except for the numerous times Katie had nudged its button to make sure she hadn't missed a text or call.

She couldn't really blame Cassidy for not checking in, but it would have been nice if she had. Yes, Katie had ruined last night by freaking out, by chickening out—she took full responsibility for that. But Cassidy could have been a bit more sensitive and understanding, couldn't she?

Just then an email came in from Marion: *Still waiting on those documents to come in for signatures.*

No problem, Katie emailed back.

They made eye contact through their respective panes of glass.

Marion quickly shot off another message. *Your hair is really getting long. Is that on purpose?*

Direct comments on Katie's appearance were a Marion specialty that would have bothered Katie far less if they were better friends. But in spite of Katie's early efforts to ply Marion with offers of Starbucks and invitations to afternoon frozen yogurt, they weren't that close. After two years of working together their conversations rarely went deeper than complaints about a broken scanner or low toner in the copy machine—and then out of nowhere, bam! Marion would blindside Katie with some shameless cheap shot about her shoes or eye shadow.

In this case, though, Marion's barb was justified. Just this morning Katie had thought to herself that she was due for a hair appointment with Vivienne. But she'd decided her split ends could go on a little longer, till she felt more ready to face Vivienne with the news of her broken engagement, not to mention everything else that had happened since.

Not on purpose, Katie wrote back to Marion, punctuated with a smiley face. Then she checked her cell phone. Still no word from Cassidy.

Katie added a few more file folders to her phone's barricade and decided to surrender. She would be the one to break. She texted Cassidy: *Any chance you're around tonight? To talk?*

Then she waited.

Nothing.

Great. This was like being thirteen all over again, when everything was so new and inexplicable and all of it felt like a secret. But it was way more enjoyable back then. Adults should not behave this way.

Of course, by refusing to go up to Cassidy's apartment, Katie had only confirmed what Cassidy already probably thought of her, which was that she was clueless and confused.

She *was* clueless and confused.

Katie understood that just because you make out with a woman one time, it doesn't mean you're gay, but what if you find yourself angling to meet up with the object of your affection the very next night in hopes that you might have a few drinks and it'll happen again?

She tapped at her phone to open Google. The cursor blinked anxiously in the search box.

After a quick glance to make sure Marion was contained behind her desk in her office across the hall, Katie typed the question into her phone: *What do lesbians do?* Before hitting the search button, she added, *to each other.*

Finger at the ready, poised to X out of whatever porno nightmare might pop up, Katie was relieved to be greeted with a barrage of lists and tips from what appeared to be semireputable sources. A few words jumped out at her as she scrolled: *oral, penetrative, anal.*

Anal? she thought. Really?

She scrolled some more. *G-spot, fisting, sex toys.* Then her phone vibrated, and she nearly fell off her chair.

It was a text back from Cassidy: *I'd really like that, but I'm going to be stuck here late tonight.*

Katie read the text three times over. Was it possible Cassidy was lying, that she was avoiding her?

She tried to evaluate the composition of this text from Cassidy's position. Straight girl flirts with you, straight girl kisses you, straight girl freaks out and goes home—and then texts you even though you've made no effort to remedy the situation.

Yeah, this was a blow-off text if she'd ever seen one. Which was fine. It was probably for the best, in fact.

Katie had tapped back to Google, to exit the page, and also clear the search from her history, when she noticed a link for a store called Babeland. She clicked on it and a banner appeared across the top of her screen that read: *Shop. Sex Info. Community. Thirty percent off all vibrators!*

She must have passed by this place a thousand times—there was a location just a few blocks from her apartment—though it wasn't surprising that it had escaped her attention. Katie often caught herself walking around her neighborhood on autopilot, anesthetized to the city's glory in a way that would have scandalized her younger self.

The homepage alone for this store terrified her, so Katie zeroed in on the "info" portion of the banner.

More info would be good. She clicked around to learn more. How could more info not be good?

The store didn't only sell toys, she noticed. It also sold books, and somehow an informational sex book seemed more wholesome and trustworthy than the dark and anonymous Internet.

If Katie was going to seek out lesbian sex facts, she might as well be sure they were of the factual variety.

It didn't mean she had to go off and actually have lesbian sex.

But she had kissed a girl. And she had liked it. And Katy Perry didn't have much more to say on the matter other than that one song, so perhaps a research trip to the sex shop was in order.

"Knock knock," Marion said as she swung open Katie's office door. "Documents are ready for signatures."

⋰♡⋱

Babeland was open till ten p.m., so Katie figured, why not swing by? She was a grown woman fully capable of entering a sex store without the excuse of shopping for a bachelorette party gag gift.

She stepped through the door like it was no big deal, like the first sight of the dildo table didn't make her want to cover her eyes.

"Hi there." A salesperson who looked like an Alison Bechdel drawing, with spiky hair and glasses, approached from behind the register. "Can I help you with anything?"

"Just looking." Katie sidled over to a nonthreatening shelf of books. She reached for a pink-and-red tome with a cover that appeared to be a minimalist depiction of two breasts and a snatch, and paged through it.

"Are you looking for anything in particular?" The salesperson had followed her to the shelf. According to her name tag, her name was Elizabeth, which struck Katie as an overtly feminine and queenly name for such a gender-neutral woman. Why not Liz or Lizzy? Maybe she had been tortured throughout middle school with taunts of *lez* or *lezzy*?

Katie held up the book. "Is this for gay women?"

Elizabeth smiled in a friendly way, perhaps because she was a gay woman, or at least a very gay-looking woman. "It's for anyone who wants to have better sex," she said.

Katie laughed much too loud. Christ, this place made her nervous. "I would like that," she said.

"Do you have a partner?" Elizabeth asked.

Katie shook her head. "I don't think so."

"Would you say you're looking to explore self-pleasure?" Elizabeth gestured toward a table of vibrators.

Katie hugged the sex book to her chest and nodded.

She followed Elizabeth to the table, not wanting to get too close to the alien-looking contraptions before her. Some were bendy and rubber with bulbous heads. Others had animal ears or wires coming out of them. She couldn't imagine where in hell on a person's body they were supposed to be applied.

"Do you already have a vibrator at home?" Elizabeth asked.

"No." Katie looked to her left and then to her right, before reaching out to pick up the biggest and most embarrassing contraption of the bunch. "This one looks like the hand blender I use to make smoothies."

"That's the Magic Wand," Elizabeth said. "It's a classic, but not for everyone and definitely not a starter vibe." She clicked it on, and its rumbly vibration made Katie jump. "You can also add on an attachment."

Elizabeth led Katie to a center table that featured a spread of dildos standing at attention like perverted wooden soldiers. Many had balls, which Katie found baffling.

Elizabeth picked up a brightly colored silicone attachment that looked like a cross between Gonzo from the Mup-
pets and a disabled elephant. She squeezed it over the head
of the wand vibrator and explained how this was an "accessory" that transformed the wand from a solely external tool
to both an external and an internal one. That was the exact
word she used, *accessory*. Like this was a simple pair of ear-
rings that you could choose to wear on the outside or inside
of your ears. "It's perfect for G-spot massage," she said.

"I squirted across the room once using that thing," a
voice from somewhere said.

Katie turned in the direction of the voice, to a woman
wearing a black leather corset and holding a whip like the
one Indiana Jones used.

"I highly recommend it," she said.

"Okay. Thank you." Katie handed the wand back to Elizabeth. "This gives me a lot to think about."

Too much to think about. What had this woman squirted
exactly? Were there fluids that Katie didn't know about?

"I can take it from here. You can go help that nice corseted
woman over there." Katie averted her attention to the near-
est distraction, which was unfortunately the army of dildos.

She picked up one that was made of textured glass. It had
icicle swirls running up its shaft. What do they call this one,
she wondered, the Anna or Elsa model? And why do they
give the damn things names? And if lesbians don't like dicks,

why shove these freakish decoys into themselves and one another? And the balls! Why?

Katie set the icicle dildo back down in its place. Maybe this was too much too fast.

She went to the register with the sex book and set it on the counter.

"Are you all set?" Elizabeth asked from where she was assisting the Squirter with a device that looked to Katie like a cattle prod.

"Yes. Just this." Katie took out her credit card as Elizabeth came around the counter to ring her up. "And this." Katie bolted back to the vibrator table, grabbed a hot-pink gadget that was only slightly embarrassing and not at all like something she could whip a smoothie in.

"The Boss Lady," Elizabeth said. "That's a great choice. It's firm yet pliant, with a tilted head for G-spot stimulation. And it even has a booster button—"

"I'm sold," Katie said, louder than she'd intended. "I mean, you don't have to sell me. I'll take it."

"Okay." Elizabeth stepped around the counter. "But that's the floor model. I have to get it for you from the back."

She disappeared, and Katie stared at her phone to avoid seeing anything or anyone else.

"You look like a Boss Lady in that fancy business suit of yours," the corseted Squirter said. She snapped a whip against the floor. "Don't forget the batteries."

❤

Katie removed her purchases from their bright blue shopping bag, then tore the bag to bright blue shreds and shoved them into the recycling. She uncorked a bottle of red wine, brought a glass to the living room, and sat across from her new book and vibrator.

Where to begin?

She slid the Boss Lady out of its black box, inserted its batteries, and switched it on. She watched it do its thing, shaking in the palm of her hand, then thrusting in the palm of her hand, then shaking and thrusting in the palm of her hand.

Katie switched off the Boss Lady and set it upon the coffee table beside her wineglass, so the two of them were standing at odds like a deviant still life. She reached for the book.

There was more nudity in its pages than she'd realized at the store, which she guessed was to be expected in a sex how-to, but these bodies looked a little too real. Had this been published before Photoshop was invented?

She flipped some more until she stumbled upon the words *lesbian fantasy*.

She took a sip of wine.

"Eighty percent of straight women have had lesbian fantasies."

She took another sip of wine and read on, hoping to get some more numbers.

Specifically, of that 80 percent, how many acted on the fantasy, and from that group, how many had given gay sex hardly any mind at all before encountering this one single lesbian?

Katie had never been a fantasizer of any kind. She was more of a planner, a doer. She was a pleaser of others—not one for exploring self-pleasure or whatever the heck Elizabeth from Babeland called it.

But Cassidy was hot. And the only other women Katie ever thought of as hot were the ones she wanted to be. Not do. Be.

It only confused her further that Cassidy was hot like a guy was hot. She'd felt almost male to Katie when she was kissing her.

Katie's doorbell rang, and she instinctively grabbed the vibrator from the table and shoved it under the couch. Someone had probably pressed the wrong bell. It happened all the time, but she still slid the book beneath the couch's cushion.

Then her phone dinged.

A text from Cassidy: *Hey, are you home? I'm at your door.*

What the hell?

Katie ran to check herself in the mirror. She was in pajama bottoms and a T-shirt. No bra. Her hair was in a ponytail.

The doorbell rang again.

Oh fuck it.

She buzzed Cassidy in and made sure the Boss Lady's hot-pink exterior wasn't visible from any angle. She opened the door and waited.

The sight of Cassidy climbing up her stairs wearing an overcoat and carrying a briefcase made her stomach do a flip.

"I know this is weird, me showing up like this." Cassidy entered and closed the door behind her. "I was in a cab and about to text you, but then I just told the driver to take me here instead. I don't know why. I just really wanted to see you."

"So you really were stuck at work," Katie said.

"Of course. What did you think?" Cassidy set down her briefcase and shook off her coat. She seemed uncharacteristically frazzled. "You said earlier that you wanted to talk?"

"I did want to talk," Katie said. "I do."

"Can we sit?" Cassidy gestured toward the couch.

Katie remained in place, standing awkwardly in front of the door. She didn't want Cassidy to sit down, not only because she feared her foot would accidently brush up against the vibrator Katie had stashed there.

"I haven't been able to stop thinking about you," Katie said.

The roiling energy Cassidy had brought into the apartment went still. "Is that a good thing or a bad thing?"

Katie wasn't sure if it was good or bad, but it was undeniable.

Cassidy took a step closer.

Katie leaned her back against the door. She waited for Cassidy to kiss her, but Cassidy didn't—she wouldn't. She would have left them suspended in midair with an inch between their lips forever if Katie hadn't reached for Cassidy and pulled her in.

That was the only green light Cassidy seemed to need to take over from there. All that nervous energy she'd arrived with came pouring out of her then. It wasn't nerves, Katie realized. It was wanting. It was need.

Cassidy steered them into Katie's bedroom, onto the bed.

"I don't know what I'm doing," Katie said.

"I am totally okay with that." Cassidy slid Katie's T-shirt up and off. Her mouth made its way down Katie's neck, across her chest.

Katie closed her eyes and let herself get lost.

TWELVE

As a rule Cassidy never cuddled after sex. It gave girls the wrong idea to hold them longer than necessary. It made them get attached.

She reminded herself of this while holding Katie, grazing her fingers up and down her arm, punch-drunk on the smell of her hair.

They were lying in the dark, but with streetlamp light coming in from the window on one side, and living room light coming in from the open door on the other, Cassidy could make out the entire space. Katie's bedroom was small, seemingly unloved, with a hodgepodge of IKEA furniture, but it was comfortable. These rough, big-box-store sheets enveloped the two of them in a warm cocoon, and the pedestrian chatter and noisy car horns from outside only added to the feeling that they were hidden away someplace softer and more secure than the outer world. If Cassidy wasn't careful she might doze off.

It was time to go, well past midnight, and Katie had been asleep now for almost half an hour.

Cassidy eyed the rumpled mound of her suit on the floor beside the bed. Her shoes she'd kicked off by the dresser. God only knew where her socks were. Carefully, she slid her arm out from under Katie, filling the empty space with a pillow, but she assumed Katie would still wake up while she was getting dressed.

"Katie," she whispered as she buttoned her shirt.

Cassidy had to go. They both had work early in the morning. Spending the night was not an option.

"I'm leaving," she tried again while buckling her belt.

Did it matter if she said goodbye? Would Katie be upset by waking up and finding her gone?

Cassidy didn't leave notes for girls to wake up to. Maybe she'd send a text a day or two later, but usually not even that. It was better to keep their expectations low right off the bat. But Cassidy was having trouble treating Katie like any other girl.

Shoes tied, good to go, Cassidy noticed an envelope on Katie's dresser, some presorted piece of junk mail from Time Warner. Not far off was a ballpoint pen.

Cassidy scribbled a quick note on the back of the envelope, *Sweet dreams. Talk to you tomorrow.—C*, and left it on Katie's nightstand.

No one could ever know about this.

-ᔜ♡ᔛ-

The next day Cassidy was a rocket, propelling herself through her work with a singular purpose—to get back to Katie.

With her suit jacket hung on the back of her chair, dress shirt sleeves rolled up to her elbows, an outside observer might have thought she'd snorted a line of coke for breakfast the way she ricocheted from office to conference room to office as the head lawyer on a new deal.

On a pit stop at the printer, she encountered her nemesis.

"Whoa, where's the fire?" Hamlin was dunk, dunk, dunking his damn Lipton tea bag in his glass mug, on his way from the office kitchen back to his desk. "Don't you know the story about the tortoise and the hare? Slow and steady wins the race."

DRINK COFFEE, Cassidy wanted to say to him.

"Did you get my email about that issue with Deutsche?" Hamlin asked, still dunking.

"I did," Cassidy said. "And I emailed you back."

"Oh, you did? Great. What did you write back?"

Cassidy homed in on the collar pin propping up Hamlin's tie knot. *YOU LOOK LIKE A WIMPY VERSION OF GORDON GEKKO*, she wanted to say.

"I'm kind of in the middle of something here." Cassidy wrested her document from the printer and stepped past him. No, not even Hamlin could bring her down today. "Maybe you can just go read the email," she said.

Back at her desk, Cassidy kept her cell phone out where she could see it as she marked up her document, jotting notes, drawing arrows, crossing out redundant words, and slashing erroneous commas. Every text Katie sent her was fuel. Every text she returned was oxygen.

The sex last night had been good, even better than Cassidy had expected, though it was hard to say why. Cassidy had done all the doing, of course. So what made it any different from all the other times with countless other women? Cassidy reflected on this while perusing an addendum to her document. It must have been how much she wanted it. How she'd been trying to fight it. Plus, their chemistry was undeniable. Cassidy had felt that right away, and it had proved true, even with Katie's tentativeness once they really got rolling, that split second when Katie seemed to almost panic—no, not panic, but stiffen. Cassidy signed off on the addendum. The way she'd had to ease Katie into it, adjust her touch, careful not to overwhelm her with anything unexpected, had only turned Cassidy on more. And then, how Katie had opened up to her—reimagining it now made Cassidy frantic. If she couldn't see Katie again tonight she might spontaneously combust.

But as the hours ticked by, their plans for dinner had to be pushed back to plans for drinks. And then plans for drinks were foiled by a last-minute client request.

Of all the nights to get stuck working late, she texted Katie at ten p.m. *Why???*

By the time Cassidy wrestled on her overcoat and headed for the elevator, Katie had already gone to bed, and she was too exhausted by her own disappointment to even swing by the Met—and that was really saying something. There were few ailments Metropolis couldn't soothe.

As she exited her office building, she checked her phone one last time to make sure Katie hadn't miraculously woken up and texted a booty call.

She had missed a text—but it was from Becky. *Where you at? Haven't seen you since I made fifty bucks off your make-out sesh at the bbq.*

Cassidy wrote back, *Just out of work. Not making it to Met tonight.*

It's dead tonight anywayz, Becky wrote. *Come to my place. I'll cook you dinner.*

Cassidy checked her watch and wrote back, *It's midnight.*

A midnight snack then.

Thanks, but I'm gonna head home. Cassidy looked up and down the street for a taxi.

Come on, Becky wrote. *I miss your prettyboy face. I'll make you my special grilled cheese . . . Just went to Murray's this afternoon . . .*

Chef Becky's grilled cheese was no joke, a week's worth of fat and calories in one sitting, but well worth it.

I'm coming, Cassidy wrote back.

You will be when you get a load of my Gruyère . . .

Don't make me change my mind. Cassidy found a cab and climbed in.

She hadn't been to Becky's in a while. Back in the day, her apartment had been a constant. Their whole crew would get wasted at the Met, pick up girls, bring them around the block in a wild parade to Becky's. Becky would cook, games would be played—spin the bottle, strip Street Fighter—and sometimes a threesome or foursome, or fivesome, sixsome, or sevensome would ensue.

The best nights, though, the ones that really stood out in Cassidy's memory, were when it was just the two of them hanging out, having a late-night food fest, passing the time like it would last forever.

It was a blast when Gina moved to town and started dating Becky—until they broke up. Then everything got messed up. Cassidy had decided that Gina needed her more than Becky did because Gina was the more broken one, and Becky understood that. But sometimes Cassidy missed how easy their friendship used to be, before all the complications.

Cassidy's taxi passed the Met just before turning the corner onto Becky's block, and she couldn't help but glance to see who might be out front. It was a reflex. No matter what time of day it was—it could be eight in the morning—if Cassidy passed the Met, her head turned. She wasn't looking for a familiar face. It was more just what people did when they happened upon their home en route to someplace else—and that's basically what the Met was to Cassidy, a second home.

Out of the car and through the front gate, Cassidy pressed the worn, familiar doorbell on Becky's building and waited to be buzzed in.

She climbed the three flights up—those same rickety wooden stairs with the same loose step that always scared her half to death—and found the apartment door open. Becky was already grating a brick of cheese into a snowy pile when she stepped inside.

"Welcome, welcome, welcome." Becky blew her a kiss. "Make yourself at home."

Becky's apartment was mostly kitchen—pots and pans hanging from the ceiling, towering stacks of giant mixing bowls, industrial shelves packed with menacing appliances, and an oven she had special-ordered. Since her brief brush with fame, the place was also littered with promotional items from her season on *Knife Fight*.

Cassidy shrugged off her coat and approached the life-size cardboard cutout of herself that Becky had displayed in the living room. In the cutout she was wearing a white blood-smeared apron and a navy blue bandana around her head. She was standing with one foot in front of the other, one arm pointing out and the other raised alongside her head, ready to throw a giant chef's knife.

Cassidy gave it a tap on the forehead. "Still have your own doppelgänger as your roommate, I see."

"I'm thinking of sending her on the road to promote the new restaurant." Becky continued to grate. "Sort of like a Flat Stanley meets Amélie's gnome, meets Guy Fieri. How do you feel about me adding prosciutto to this?"

"Go crazy." Cassidy untied her oxfords and kicked them off.

"Want a drink?"

"I do if this is an intervention," Cassidy said.

"Help yourself to the good scotch." Becky pointed with her knife toward her bar cart.

"Damn it. I knew this sandwich was going to cost me." Cassidy trudged over to the cart to pour herself a glass of something strong. "Let me guess, you want to talk to me about Katie."

"I like Katie," Becky said. "I'm a big fan, in fact. She's our age. She's not married to a man. She's beautiful. Smart."

"She's not that straight," Cassidy interjected.

"Smart. I said *smart*."

"You were going to say *straight* next." Drink in hand, Cassidy plopped down on the couch across from cardboard Becky.

Becky's pile of grated cheese was now a small mountain. "What I was going to say next was *sweet*. And anyway I saw her kissing you. I'm not buying it that she's all that straight."

"Gina doesn't like her," Cassidy said.

"Gina's only trying to protect you. She can see how much you like this girl, and she doesn't want you to get hurt. Personally, I think Katie can be good for you." Becky sliced her way through a thick loaf of Pullman bread. "I've known you for what, seven years now?"

"That can't be right." Cassidy lay horizontally across the couch, resting her drink on her stomach.

"It is right." Becky slapped a hunk of butter on one of the slices of bread. "You were just out of NYU when we met; you hadn't even started law school. Now you're thirty. I turn thirty next year. You, me, and Dahlia, now we're like the goddamn elders. Of our original group, have you not noticed that we're the only three left? Everyone else either aged out, coupled off, or got sober."

"Is this supposed to make me want to kill myself?" Cassidy said. "If so, you're doing a great job."

Becky swirled some olive oil around her frying pan. "I'm just making the point that for years I've watched you fuck around with every piece of tail that stepped into that bar. I've seen girls throw drinks in your face, throw glasses at the wall beside your head, throw themselves at me just to spite you. And you'd just continue on, all la-di-da, barely flinching. For a while there I was convinced you were actually a sociopath."

"Where you going with this, Chef?"

Becky covered her sizzling sandwich and took a step back from the stove. "Even the girls you dated for a few months, it was obvious it wouldn't last. And the ones you could have had something real with, you never gave them the time of day. But Katie's different. I can see it in the way you look at her."

"Oh, give me a goddamn break."

"Go ahead, pretend you're playing it cool. Your act doesn't work on me." Becky flipped her sandwich and re-covered the pan. "You forget that I know what's going on below the façade. I know how soft you are beneath there."

"Okay, you know what?" Cassidy sat up. "Just because I cried that one time we did shrooms doesn't mean you can see into my soul."

"Ha. I'd forgotten about that. But you're wrong. I did see

into your soul that day." Becky slid the sandwich out of the pan onto her cutting board. She sliced it in half with a giant knife. "We're not so different, you and me. Sure, you're taller, thinner, richer, and more handsome, but you're just as messed up on the inside as I am. And deep down you know that no matter how hard you work out, how healthy you eat, how expensive your skin care regimen is, no amount of up-keep is stopping time." Becky slid both halves of the sand-wich onto a plate. "I think it's time for both of us to start thinking about the future."

"Is this seriously why you lured me over tonight?" Cas-sidy said.

Becky walked the plate over to Cassidy and set it down on the table in front of her. "Eat these carbs. I promise they'll make you feel better."

"I felt fine till I came here."

"I have some bad news." Becky grabbed the bottle of good scotch off her bar cart and then joined Cassidy on the couch.

"Oh fuck," Cassidy said. "Who's dead?"

Becky unscrewed the bottle and refilled Cassidy's glass. "Nobody's dead."

Cassidy let her gooey sandwich sit untouched on her plate. "Whatever it is, just say it, because you're scaring the hell out of me right now."

"Metropolis is closing," Becky said.

"Again?" Cassidy exhaled with relief. "Because of the board of health? How long will it be this time?"

"No. I mean permanently. Forever."

"I don't understand."

"The lease is up, and the building got sold to developers. They want to convert it to a mixed-use space, retail and apartments, something like that. Dahlia said something about air rights? I don't even know."

"Are you making this shit up right now?"

"I wish I were."

Cassidy's stomach dropped. "There's got to be something we can do."

"I don't think so," Becky said. "These developers don't want a bar there. They don't want nightlife. They want a live/work environment for people with a lot of money and sticks up their asses. It's kind of amazing the Met has survived this long."

"It's just not right." Cassidy leaned forward, put her head in her hands. "How soon is this all happening?"

"End of the month."

"End of the month?!" Cassidy's head shot back up. "This month? Are you kidding?"

"Eat your sandwich," Becky said. "It's getting cold."

THIRTEEN

Lying naked in Cassidy's arms felt similar to lying naked in a man's arms, but the feeling of Cassidy's bare skin on Katie's was completely different. It was softer, smoother, and Cassidy smelled cleaner than any man Katie had ever been with. This shouldn't have been surprising given Cassidy's elaborate grooming rituals. Katie had seen her bathroom products, her body lotions and facial moisturizers. Of course her skin was soft. Of course she smelled amazing in a way not even the gayest gay man could compete with.

Having sex with Cassidy felt similar to having sex with a man, too, but also entirely different.

After sliding Katie's pajama bottoms down and off, Cassidy stood at the edge of the bed and undressed herself. Katie watched her unbutton her shirt and throw it to the floor, then pull what looked like a neutral-colored sports bra up and over her head. She let Katie look at her for a few seconds before stepping out of her suit pants. When she climbed back on top of Katie, her gray boxer-briefs clinging to her thighs against Katie's own low-rise bikini underwear didn't freak Katie out—it felt familiar. It felt sexy.

Katie was hyper aware of Cassidy's body against her own, the curve of her chest and stomach, the angle of her hip-bones. It was Cassidy's hands that Katie lost track of, her confident hands, and her warm mouth.

It ended faster than she wanted it to. Before she even re-alized it was happening, she was digging her fingers into Cassidy's back, holding her there for just a moment before pushing her away. Then she lay flat, covering her face.

"Are you okay?" Cassidy asked.

Katie nodded, staring straight up at the ceiling. "I'm not sure how this works," she said. "Am I supposed to do you now?"

"No." Cassidy wrapped her arm around her. "Now you just relax."

Cassidy helped her relax by holding her close, grazing her fingers up and down Katie's arm, inducing her into a trance state like a hypnotist dangling a watch before her eyes.

It was already the middle of the night when Katie rolled over and Cassidy was gone. She remained still for a few minutes, unsure if Cassidy had left or simply gone to the bathroom. If she heard a flush or running water, Katie decided she would close her eyes and feign sleep—play possum. Because snoozing possums never had to account for themselves—they weren't expected to answer questions or have appropriate reactions, or not freak out for the benefit of the same-sex possum they had just hastily mated with.

After a few more minutes Katie sat up, saw Cassidy's clothes were gone from the floor, and then noticed a note on her nightstand.

Sweet dreams. Talk to you tomorrow.

Of course they would, but what would Katie say? That she didn't know what to call this? That she wasn't sure if it was a crazy rebound, an uncharacteristic acting-out, or a sexual awakening? Or if it was an identity crisis. Or a mistake.

This isn't me, she might say. *This isn't who I am.* But did she know who she was when no one was watching?

The next morning at work Katie kept going to the bathroom to check herself in the mirror. Was there a shine to her eyes that gave her away? Did the color in her cheeks betray her? What about her mouth? Did her lips shimmer in a new wanton way? She brought her face right up to the glass for closer examination, certain that she was somehow broadcasting a change.

Because she did feel changed somehow, like she was hiding something unclean, which was of course ridiculous.

Why should it matter that Cassidy was female? How outmoded it was to feel guilty. But when Cassidy texted to say she was stuck working late and their dinner plans would have to get pushed to after-dinner drinks, the knot that had been pulled taut in Katie's stomach came undone. She responded with nonchalance. *No problem. I know how it is. Keep me posted.* But her physical relief was undeniable.

Katie stopped for groceries on her way home and bought ingredients for her mother's lemon roasted chicken. She craved its familiarity and the smell of comfort it would fill her apartment with. It was one of the first dishes her mother had taught her to prepare, step by step.

"You'll cook this for a boy one day," her mother had told her. "And he'll think you're a knockout, because he'll have no clue how easy it is to make."

Of course Katie had never gotten the chance to dazzle Paul Michael with her roasting skills, because he didn't eat meat, or butter for that matter, but it remained her go-to recipe whenever she needed to self-soothe.

Katie squeezed the juice from two lemons like everything was just as it had always been. She removed the giblets and neck from the chicken like her entire life hadn't suddenly come into question.

It was done. She and Cassidy had slept together. Katie should have been focusing on what was going to happen next, not existentially but logistically.

Except that sleeping with Cassidy had been like putting

on a pair of glasses. It was impossible now to not review all of her previous relationships through this sharper lens.

Was she gay now? Had she always been? Did this mean she should go back and revise her memories of past friendships, reappraise the intensity of her feelings for her former best girlfriends?

Maddie in high school. Hannah in college.

Amy was never really a best friend, even before she ran off with Katie's fiancé. She only earned that title by default, by being the least insufferable of the crowd that came with Paul Michael. Early on, when Katie sat down to her first brunch with them, they all struck her as something out of a Woody Allen film, which was not a compliment in her mind. Amy was the only one who seemed unpretentious enough to be harmless.

Amy wasn't dumb, per se, but she lacked a filter enough to be refreshing. She was the kind of girl who would rather have been the butt of the joke than have no one at the table paying attention to her—which gave Katie an out once in a while. Like when Katie asked their brunch waiter what a bialy was, and the whole table burst out laughing, Amy immediately volunteered that she too wished she knew nothing of the existence of this poor man's bagel that'd give you onion breath all day. Or when Lillian, of Lincoln and Lillian, asked if Kentucky was in the South or the Midwest— Katie gave the most polite answer she could muster through clenched teeth, which was that it was a Southern state with Midwestern influences, but it was Amy who broke the tension by saying, "Whaaat? How is that possible?" Katie offered its close proximity to Ohio, Illinois, and Indiana as the reason. To which Amy replied, "Kentucky is near Ohio?"

Considering it now, this nightmare first brunch with the friends should have sent Katie running, but at the time it gave her an odd sense of comfort. She had sat down at that table feeling like a fish out of water, or rather like a big fish from a small sea that was suddenly a newly self-conscious little fish, encumbered by how rarely she'd left the three-hundred-mile radius of her home state. Meanwhile, these people literally didn't know other states existed. They couldn't find them on a map. To Paul Michael's friends, there was Manhattan, a little bit of Brooklyn, the Hamptons part of Long Island, and that was basically it. They were no less encumbered by failing to leave their comfort zone than she was—the only difference was that their comfort zone involved bialys.

Katie remembered telling herself that this was what she had come to the city for, to expose herself to such foreign mysteries as a Polish breakfast roll. Sure, Paul Michael's group could make her cringe, but she still wanted to know them, to understand them, to learn to laugh with them. And Amy would be her ally.

But Katie had never felt a deep closeness to Amy—that

feeling of connection and rightness and always wanting to be with this person–ness that she'd had almost instantly with both Maddie and Hannah.

Katie placed the chicken in a roasting pan. She smeared it with butter and herbs, doused it with lemon juice.

Maddie had been like the sister Katie yearned for growing up. From the moment she moved in up the street from Katie in tenth grade, they were inseparable. They looked alike, dressed alike. They made each other brave and needed nobody else.

Katie had met Hannah when they pledged the same sorority during freshman year at UT. They were fortuitously paired together for quiz night—a tormenting process during which recruits were tested game-show style on their sorority's history, the names of national leaders, and important details about all the current members.

Katie and Hannah, two natural-born test takers with exceptional memorization skills, were a dream team, blowing their competition out of the water. Their fate was sealed that night. From then on, they were each other's number one, and full-fledged sisters for life.

Until Katie blew their relationship up, just like she'd done to Maddie a few years earlier.

Katie broke into a sweat at the memory of it now, how she was driven crazy when each of them betrayed her trust, her fidelity.

When Maddie changed her mind about going to UT with Katie and followed her boyfriend to Ohio State instead.

When Hannah abandoned Katie for Boyfriend Land in the middle of junior year.

Katie had refused to forgive either of them. How could she? Even with Justin or Travis, or whatever boy happened to be in her life, Katie had still managed to keep her priorities straight. She was utterly loyal to her best girlfriends, and she expected no less in return.

Katie sprinkled salt and pepper over the top of the chicken.

She began to wonder—did she love them? Maddie and Hannah. In more than just a friendship way. Was that what all the fuss was about?

I'm a really good friend, Katie always thought. *I put my girlfriends first. If you wanna be my lover, you gotta get with my friends.* But Katie's bordering-on-obsessive adoration of Maddie and Hannah must have, all along, been about wanting more. Katie remembered her illogical constant need of them as almost painful, agonizing with the possibility that this time maybe they'd get there, that some anonymous expectation would be filled in such quantity and quality that it would be enough.

If Katie had loved Maddie and Hannah, did she ever truly love Paul Michael?

Her sex life with Paul Michael had always been fine. Sex with boys had always been fine. And not once had Katie felt physically attracted to Maddie or Hannah, or at least not that she realized. She just always wanted them near her.

Katie cut tiny grooves into the lemons that would be stuffed into the chicken with her chopping knife.

It was useful to think of it this way: if she were playing a game of Fuck/Marry/Kill, Katie would have absolutely chosen to fuck Paul Michael but marry Maddie or Hannah.

Though taking into consideration last night, and the way for days now her body had been behaving like its own animal . . .

Oh dear lord. Katie let go of her chopping knife and wiped her brow with the back of her hand. She'd forgotten all about the salacious book still hidden in her couch's seat cushion and the hot-pink Boss Lady vibrator lying somewhere beneath the couch like a forgotten dog toy.

Katie went to the living room and got down on all fours to retrieve both items, then carried them into the bedroom like contraband. The vibrator went into her nightstand drawer, shoved all the way to the back. The book she stood with for a moment, while her mind spun out.

If fucking, marrying, and killing Cassidy all at once was a possibility—then she had no idea what to do next.

Forget her lemon roasted chicken.

Katie brought the book into bed with her. Studying for a test had always calmed her. It was why she'd always achieved straight A's.

Okay, she thought. Let's do this.

She switched on her bedside lamp for some proper task lighting and opened the book to chapter 8: *"Lesbian Sex: A How-to."*

The chapter's section headings indicated that she should not skip ahead but start at the beginning. The introduction on "techniques and positions," for example, seemed way more approachable than the latter section "Fisting Safely."

Katie was engrossed in the section titled "Licking: Also Known as Cunnilingus" when she got a text from Cassidy saying she was still unsure when she could leave work.

It was already so late. Who were they kidding?

She texted Cassidy back: *That's okay. I think I should go to sleep soon anyway. Zzz.*

But now she was all hot and bothered from the reading she'd done—the obscene bodily feats she'd spent the last hour imagining, step-by-X-rated-step, in her mind's eye. She was relieved to not be seeing Cassidy tonight, but with all these images fresh in her mind she needed—something. Some kind of release.

Katie considered her nightstand, and the vibrator lying dormant inside.

This was all too much.

She should cook.

She should eat.

Katie reached over to the nightstand, opened the drawer, and felt around until she had the Boss Lady in hand.

Then she clicked off her bedside lamp.

On Wednesday evening Katie had already closed out all the tabs on her computer and was about to apply her leaving-the-office coat of lipstick when Marion knocked on her door.

"The call with Merrill just got moved up to tomorrow morning," Marion said. "So the partners are going to need that draft by sometime tonight."

Katie re-capped her lipstick. "You're kidding."

"I guess we can't really complain. We haven't worked past two in a while." Marion pulled down her eyeglasses from on top of her head onto her weary eyes. She was thirty-seven and didn't look a day under forty-five thanks to nights like this. "Your hair just keeps getting longer," she said.

Katie stared into Marion's eyeglasses. Guilty as charged. She was still avoiding getting her hair cut because she was still avoiding Vivienne.

"Yes," Katie said. "It does just keep getting longer. Hair is funny that way."

Once Marion was out of earshot Katie let out a few choice words—and then picked up her phone to text Cassidy.

Another night would have to go by without their seeing each other.

Another night of thwarted efforts.

Looking down at her and Cassidy's most recent texts back and forth, Katie considered the possibility that divine intervention was keeping them apart. This was old thinking and she knew it, the kind her mother and grandmother resorted to in times of frustration. If it rained on their Fourth of July picnic or if there was traffic on I-64 making them late to the Taste of Derby Festival, somehow it was always God's will. Katie had long since decided, quietly, on her own, that sometimes stuff just happened for no reason.

And yet the thought still haunted her as she texted Cassidy, *So sorry. Have to pull an all-nighter.*

Katie urged her attention back onto her work and reopened all the necessary tabs on her computer. She searched the file labeled *Merrill* for where she'd left off in her notes and switched on Track Changes.

A thought entered Katie's mind then. A picture really, or pictures—a multitude of nude, un-Photoshopped bodies. Page after page of them.

The memory alone made her sort of . . . *Wet* was such a crass word in this context. Lubricated?

Excited, maybe. Beneath her desk, Katie uncrossed and recrossed her legs.

She might not get to see Cassidy tonight. But she would still go home to bed—and her nightstand.

If this was her out, though—having to work late via divine intervention—surely it wasn't God's will for her to go home and cuddle up to the vibrator she'd bought at a sex shop. Old thinking or not, did that seem like something the real Katie Daniels would do? Katie the good girl, eager to please, obedient daughter. Or, in more recent years, the hard-working, striving-to-fit-in country-girl-at-heart in the big city. None of those labels were 100 percent right. So who was to say *sexually awakened, vibrator-owning possible lesbian* would suit Katie any better?

Her phone chimed with a text back from Cassidy: *I understand, but I was really hoping to see you tonight.* Then it chimed again with an immediate follow-up: *The Met's closing. It's a total disaster. Could use your moral support!*

Whaaat? Katie replied. *Closing for good?*

I'm afraid so, Cassidy wrote.

That's terrible, Katie began, and then paused. She was ultra self-conscious of the ellipses on Cassidy's screen revealing that she had halted midthought, her ambivalence made visible by three little dots. *If by chance I get out earlier than expected,* she continued, *I'll try to come by.*

Try was good. Try was always a safe bet. It gave Katie an out just in case.

FOURTEEN

Metropolis felt like a funeral. Gina was hunched over, elbows on knees, puffing on a cigarette. Becky lingered over a spread of comfort food she'd laid out on the pool table, a tray of baked ziti, garlic bread, and an extra-large serving bowl of Caesar salad. Even Dahlia had come out from behind the bar to just sit with them and drink.

"Go ahead," she called out to the gaggle of confused out-of-towners looking to order. "Leave your money on the bar. Or don't. It doesn't matter anymore."

Off to the side of it all was Cassidy, lounging on her stool, still in her work clothes, shirtsleeves rolled up. Like her friends, she was having trouble grasping the reality of life without Metropolis, but unlike her friends she was doing it quietly.

"Who are these new owners?" Gina asked. "Who was the old owner?"

"Some guy," Dahlia said. "He's a broker or something. He doesn't even live in New York. And now he's sold the building to some other guy who's also a broker or something. It's all just an investment to him."

"Which him is that now?" Becky asked.

Dahlia shrugged. "Both."

Cassidy stayed silent. Nobody was more attached to the Met than she was, which was why her first reaction when she'd woken up this morning was to try to single-handedly rescue the bar herself. She would have liked just about now to lean back on her barstool and calmly, without fanfare, assert, *I took care of it*. To reveal that she'd saved the day by throwing money at the problem. Be the hero. Accept their thanks but shrug off their praise, say, *It was nothing*.

But this morning's due diligence had only reinforced the worst. The deal was done, it was done privately, and there was nothing Cassidy could do but accept it.

"Maybe Cassidy can negotiate with the fuckers," Gina said. "Rent out just this space, as an investment, give it to Dahlia to run."

Cassidy looked up.

They were all looking at her, eager for her reaction.

"Do you have any idea how much this space would rent for?" she said.

Their faces all dropped at once.

Cassidy did in fact know. She also knew how the building would be gutted and rebuilt, how the ground floor would become retail space, one more bullshit store filled with pointlessness, and luxury apartments floating above. But why tell these guys about that now? The pain that came from learning the truth, of her trying and failing—it would be worse somehow if they knew.

"Becky," Cassidy said. "You said it yourself. There's no negotiating with these guys. They're set on converting the building to some kind of mixed-use development."

"What the fuck is mixed use?" Gina flicked her spent cigarette onto the floor. "Why does everyone keep saying that? What's more mixed use than this?" She gestured at the room. "Where else can you find a bigger mix of age and race and class—and genders? This is about as mixed use as a place can get. That's the whole point."

Gina patted around her pockets for her pack of cigarettes and pulled out a fresh one. "We're just not the right mix, I guess, which is bullshit. I say we protest."

"If big bucks over here can't buy our way out of this," Dahlia said, "I don't think a freak parade of us out front holding up signs is going to move the needle much."

Gina lit her cigarette with a match. "I'll chain myself to the goddamn Erotic Photo Hunt machine if I have to."

"I just can't believe this is it." Becky reached for a hunk

of garlic bread off the pool table spread and bit off its end. "Every inch of this place holds a memory. Over there was where I slow-danced with that girl dressed as Diana Ross after my first Pride parade. That was where I was standing when the great beer-spitting contest of 2012 broke out. In that corner there was where I was sitting the night gay marriage was legalized and watched three separate proposals. Remember that, Cassidy?"

Cassidy nodded.

"Hey, Dahlia." Gina pointed with her cigarette. "There's an unidentified bodysuit-wearing hottie at the bar looking for the bartender."

Dahlia handed off her glass of whiskey to Cassidy. "Duty calls."

"I'm calling dibs on striped-bodysuit girl," Becky said.

Gina scoffed. "You don't stand a chance with bodysuit girl. She's way too baby-got-back for your baby back ribs."

Becky squared her shoulders to Gina. She was wearing a T-shirt she'd designed for her butcher shop that featured the slogan *Come for the tail, stay for the head.*

"I'll have you know," Becky said, "I once shared an intimate moment with a certain well-known fitness guru in the greenroom of the *Today* show."

Gina blew a stream of gray smoke in Becky's direction. "Doug the Pug hardly counts as a fitness guru."

"Go ahead and make fun." Becky tightened the knot on

her purple bandana. "But I guarantee that she, who will remain nameless out of respect for the closeted, is coming right to me on her next cheat day." Becky smiled in bodysuit girl's direction. "And anyway, I met Doug the Pug on *Good Morning America*."

"Earth to Cassidy." Gina waved her hand in front of Cassidy's eyes. "Care to get in on this bodysuit-girl game?"

"I already called dibs!" Becky screamed out.

"You can have her," Cassidy said. "I'm not interested."

Gina picked a fleck of tobacco or baked ziti from her teeth. "Not interested 'cause you're goddamn pussy-whipped. Not even. Katie-whipped is more like it."

"Wrong," Cassidy said. "I'm not interested because I hooked up with that girl at Cherry Grove last summer."

Becky shrugged her shoulders. "Lucky for me I've never been opposed to scooping up your sloppy seconds."

Cassidy swallowed down the remaining whiskey in Dahlia's glass and tried to tune everyone out.

Becky's words from last night were still rolling around her mind, helping to darken her mood. Becky had been right; there was no stopping time. And there was no sense denying it—Cassidy was aging out of her lifestyle. She and Becky and Dahlia had become the goddamn elders of this bar, and now even that had reached its shelf life.

Looking around now at the pockets of girls scattered throughout tonight's murk, a good half of them were familiar—girls Cassidy had either slept with or briefly dated. Some remained friends; others refused to speak her name. None had left a mark. She had cared about each of them enough, enjoyed them while they remained easy and ego boosting, while they fit effortlessly into her clockwork life without disruption beyond their designated groove, and then she released them when they got complicated. That was all she had to offer. She never pretended otherwise, and she never apologized. She was crystal clear from beginning to end that she wasn't looking for anything more.

But then Cassidy had met Katie. And now she couldn't unmeet her.

Maybe they'd met just in the nick of time. Maybe meeting Katie was a blessing, even though Cassidy didn't believe in blessings, or a gift from the god she'd also never believed in—the god who, if he did exist, Cassidy was pretty sure didn't believe in her.

Dear lord. That's what Katie would say to that. She was always letting a *Dear lord* slip from her lips whenever she was shocked or frustrated by something. The expression should have imparted a sense of fear in Cassidy as a card-carrying heathen, or at the very least, concern. She and Katie never spoke of it, but whether the *Dear lord*s were less prayer and more Southern verbal tic, Katie must have been raised as a good Christian girl. And that was a lot for Cassidy to be up against. The strict notions of right and wrong, of virtue versus sin—the conformity religion required was more than Katie could be expected to defy. It was all too difficult to undo. Just like Cassidy, in spite of her efforts, could never fully undo the casual traumas of her own upbringing. She didn't have to be raised with religion to absorb the disapproval of the adults around her; their notions of what about her was to be encouraged and what should be stifled.

Growing up, Cassidy was somehow always bordering on offensive, on problematic. *Spoiled* was what they called her when she threw tantrums as a child over the baby dolls and jewelry sets she received in lieu of Matchbox cars and action figures. *Stubborn* was what she was when she quit the tennis team over the regulation tennis dress requirement. Now she was selfish, distant, thankless, unwilling to see her parents more than a couple of times a year even though they lived less than five miles away. They loved her, her mother and father, but they would never understand her. Empathy was not a prevailing family trait. Civility, sure. Decorum, yes. Class, always. But Cassidy's parents didn't want to know her better because deep down they'd have preferred she were different, that she fit in their world more tolerably.

Fine. Cassidy didn't need them anyway. Here in this hotbox of smoke and sweat, filled with bodies just like hers, that defied all categorization, that no label or slur could suitably contain—here Cassidy was home. Here Cassidy didn't only fit; she triumphed. She wasn't merely tolerated; she was desired. The bar did this, Cassidy realized, which was why she'd held it so close for so long.

So if Cassidy was aging out of the bar scene, where was she aging to?

Toward Katie? She and Katie might as well have been different species. And yet, Cassidy couldn't fend off the surge of affection she felt for Katie every time she let out a *Dear lord* or *Bless her heart* or some other adorable, if not vaguely religious, thing. Cassidy couldn't talk herself out of the debilitating disappointment she experienced when she read Katie's text canceling tonight's plans.

Her own text back oozed neediness. *I understand*, Cassidy wrote, *but I was really hoping to see you tonight.*

And as if that weren't bad enough, she sent the clingiest follow-up text in the history of clingy follow-up texts about the Met closing. *Could use your moral support?* What the hell was that overeager bullshit?

Of course Katie's response was noncommittal. Cassidy wouldn't have wanted to see her own sorry ass tonight either.

"Yo, check it out, fight club, fight club." Gina jumped up onto her tippy toes trying to get a better look across the room.

"Wrestling already?" Becky said. "It isn't even one yet."

Cassidy followed Gina and Becky's lead and stood up to better see the other end of the bar, where the girls were pushing and shoving. As always, just enough space had cleared around them to give everyone a ringside view. These two had gone at it before, the long-limbed girl with dark hair, who Cassidy believed was Native American, and the scrappier, short-haired girl everyone called Biscuit.

Down they went, to the filthy floor, grappling.

Cassidy tried to imagine this spectacle through Katie's eyes. How would Cassidy explain it to her? That it was part sport, part revenge. All in good fun, but the bruises were real. That it was as passive as it was aggressive—these two duking it out probably loved the same girl, or had gotten hurt by the same girl, and so they tried to hurt each other. Because twisting, squeezing, rolling, punching, was some-how less brutal than addressing the real problem head on, with words.

It was for the best that Katie wasn't likely to show. Cassidy took a step back and ditched her drink on the pool table. She wasn't even sure she wanted to be standing here right now.

It was a fidgety, sleepless night, but Cassidy must have dozed off eventually, because early the next morning she shot up in bed, heart racing, in a cold sweat.

She looked around her bedroom, took in her surround-ings to get ahold of where she was, who she was, what day it was. Had she been dreaming? And if so, when did the dream begin, and where did it end?

Her phone was in its rightful place, beside the lamp on her nightstand. She took it in hand and pressed it awake. While she scrolled through the morning news, she continued to take stock. She hadn't brought anyone home. She hadn't gone home with anyone else. She hadn't had sex in or just outside a bar. She hadn't even bought a girl a drink. Not last night or the night before.

Was that the source of this ache in her chest? Or was it that she couldn't fathom any more time passing before she could see Katie again?

She began typing a message to Katie before she could change her mind.

Weekend getaways were for couples. Cassidy never took a girl away unless it was to circumvent a nosy spouse or girlfriend, to keep from getting caught with someone else's other half.

Let's go away this weekend, she wrote, and then waited.

FIFTEEN

·······················

Katie woke up to Cassidy's text, read it, rubbed her eyes, and read it again.

Let's go away this weekend.

She sat up in bed and stared out at the morning light through her curtainless bedroom window, unable to will her fingers to text back a reply.

Leaving the city with Cassidy seemed like a surefire way for Katie to trap herself in a situation she wouldn't be able to get out of if she wanted to. Weekend getaways didn't make for easy escape plans.

Katie climbed out of her sheets one bare foot at a time and carried her phone to the kitchen. There she was met with the onslaught of Tuesday night's dirty dishes still lingering in their caked-on grease. She pushed aside her cutting board and a few dried-up lemon rinds to clear a place on the counter for her phone.

Yawning, moving at a snail's pace, she pulled a mug from her cabinet and poured herself a hot cup of coffee. She drank it standing up, still half-asleep.

They would probably have fun, if they went away together. It didn't have to be some huge commitment. What was she so afraid of? Why was she considering her escape options when Cassidy was obviously focused, as usual, on enjoyment—on simply having a good time?

It didn't have to be some weekend sexcapade either. The two of them hadn't even had a real conversation since they'd slept together. Maybe that night was just a one-off, a one-time indiscretion. Maybe Cassidy would say, *Hey, it's good we got that out of the way; now we can really be friends.*

Maybe that's what Katie should say—that whatever it was that had had her all hot and bothered since they'd met was finally out of her system.

It wasn't out of her system, but she could say it was.

Or she could say nothing at all. Katie understood Cassidy well enough by now to know she had too much pride to push. If Katie pretended the whole thing had never happened, her money was on Cassidy's leaving it alone.

Besides, Cassidy seemed to have lots of women at her disposal—she didn't need to add Katie to her collection. She could probably take or leave ever sleeping with Katie again.

So what was the harm in taking a trip? A trip might be just the thing they needed to work out all the kinks—no, to work out all the knots in their relationship.

Katie picked up her phone from the countertop and texted back, *Where'd you have in mind?*

There. She felt better already.

While waiting for Cassidy's reply, she opened the fridge and there sat her lemon roasted chicken in its juicy roasting pan. Katie yanked a piece off the bird with her fingers, closed the fridge, and ate it leaning against the counter.

Snacking on cold chicken at seven in the morning while wearing nothing but underwear and a T-shirt was something you could only really do when you lived alone. She had forgotten about such perks.

Her phone chimed with a text then, and Katie wiped her fingers on her bare thighs before picking it up.

Anywhere, Cassidy had written. *I'll take you anywhere you want to go.*

Katie brought her phone and her coffee cup to the table and sat, hugging her knees to her chest.

Where did she want to go? It was an essential question.

The problem was, Katie wasn't so great at knowing where she wanted to go. Keeping up on places to go and things to do was Paul Michael's domain. He and his group had such strong opinions on what constituted cool, Katie had figured out early on that it was better for her not to try to make suggestions. She could still hear their voices in her head. *That restaurant is so cheesy, that bar is so basic, that music festival, that hotel, that city is so over.*

Katie chuckled to think of it now, and that was probably a healthy sign. It was better to find it funny, the preposterousness of her trying to fit in with them, than to mourn her wasted effort or agonize over her misjudgment.

The caffeine was starting to kick in, thank goodness. The morning jitters Katie always woke up with began to settle, and the world—even her cluttered kitchen—took on a kinder hue of bearability. Her thoughts started coming to her with more clarity, better light.

She asked herself again, where did she want to go?

What Katie had truly been longing for was to go riding. She missed how free and alive she felt while riding a horse.

But how would Cassidy react if Katie recommended going to some ranch upstate? Would she think horseback riding was unsophisticated, that a ranch trip was bumpkinish?

Katie couldn't really see Cassidy reacting that way. In fact, all evidence pointed toward the opposite. Cassidy seemed to enjoy the moments when Katie's accent broke through, or when she laughed too loud or cussed with gusto. Not once had Katie felt self-conscious around Cassidy or like she needed to restrain herself in some way.

So screw it.

Katie spun off her chair, went to the fridge, opened it,

and pulled off one more shred of chicken. The time for pretending to be someone she wasn't—someone supposedly better and more refined—was over. Cassidy wasn't one to try to smooth down Katie's rough edges. She didn't care if Katie wasn't perfect.

Cassidy herself was a living, breathing fuck-you to appearances, a walking middle finger to doing anything just because someone told her to. How else could she make her way through the world otherwise?

It was downright liberating to be around. Katie swallowed the last of her coffee and reached for her phone. The decision was made. They would go. And she would pick out the place herself.

SIXTEEN

I still don't understand why you can't come out tonight."
Gina plopped down onto Cassidy's bed, bowl and fork in
hand. "Especially now that we know our nights at the Met
are numbered."

Cassidy stuffed a pair of socks into an overnight bag. "I
told you. We're leaving at the crack of early tomorrow morning. Can you please go eat that in the kitchen?"

"You're making me eat quinoa, the least you can do is let
me ingest it on your bed. Explain to me again where the hell
you're going."

"Horseback riding." Cassidy debated between two nearly
identical chambray button-downs, holding one up against
herself in the mirror, then the other. "It's like a ranch or
something upstate. I wanted to take her away for the week-

end and this is what she chose. She's from Kentucky, she likes horses. What do you want from me?"

"What is up with you and this girl, C?"

"Nothing is up with me and this girl," Cassidy said. "I just like her."

"Enough to go to some fucking dude ranch? You know there's going to be dust there, and dirt, and mud, and flies. You're doing all this—for what?"

Cassidy chose the shirt in her right hand, freed it from its hanger, and folded it into a neat square. "I like spending time with her."

"Just tell me one thing." Gina fished through her quinoa bowl to locate a chunk of chicken. "Has she laid a finger on you yet?"

"Would you say raw denim is the way to go?" Cassidy asked. "Or would a cotton-blend jean allow for more flexibility?"

"That's a no," Gina said. "And it's gonna stay a no."

Cassidy examined her footwear choices. "It's not about the sex to me."

"But it's *only* about the sex to her." Gina set down her bowl on Cassidy's nightstand. "Until she gets it out of her system and meets a nice boy."

"Can't you just let me enjoy this? This isn't my first straight girl."

"But this is your first rodeo."

"Cute," Cassidy said.

Gina moved to the bed's edge and brought her feet to the floor. "Look. We both know none of those other girls meant squat to you. Are you seriously telling me you're not falling for this one?"

"Fine." Cassidy threw her hands up at her sides. "I'm falling for her, okay? Of course I am. I don't want to spend my weekend riding horses! But I think she might be falling for me, too."

Gina shook her head. "For someone so smart, C, I swear sometimes you've got shit for brains."

⚘

Cassidy pulled up to Katie's apartment building in the silver Dodge Ram pickup she'd rented for the occasion. She honked the horn at Katie out front, exhilarated by the sight of her snug flannel and blue jeans, her brown boots up to her knees, and her ponytail gleaming in the sun.

Katie approached the truck, opened the passenger-side door, and hoisted herself inside. "You rented us a pickup? Where do you think we're driving to?"

"Too much?" Cassidy asked.

"Nah. It's kind of great." Katie buckled her seat belt. "I lost my virginity in the back of a truck just like this."

Cassidy pulled away from the curb, antsy to break free from the city street traffic for the open road. Since they'd slept together, she had longed for this release from the late nights at their hectic jobs and the torture of separation, this escape into the wild.

"I see you tried to wear your most rugged outfit." Katie leaned over to inspect Cassidy's ensemble. "But I'm pretty sure Chelsea boots are supposed to stay in Chelsea."

"You look nice," Cassidy said. "You've got sort of a farmer's-daughter look going on."

"You like it?"

"I do." Cassidy returned her eyes to the traffic ahead. "So what was his name?"

"Who?"

"The boy you gave it up to in the back of a pickup truck."

Katie laughed. "Justin Barnes, quarterback of the state-champion Lafayette Generals."

"Christ," Cassidy said. "Was he as milk-fed as he sounds?"

"Oh yeah. He could have been the poster boy for the milk-does-a-body-good campaign." Katie reached into a plastic bag at her feet. "But it's crazy to think of it now, how I planned it for months ahead of time." She pulled a pumpernickel bagel out of the bag and held it up for Cassidy to see. "Want one? I've got butter and cream cheese."

"To give him your virginity?" Cassidy waved off the bagel. "You planned that out?"

Katie tore off a piece of bagel and popped it into her

mouth. "On prom night in the back of his truck, under the stars."

"Sounds romantic," Cassidy said.

"I thought so." Katie switched on the radio. "I remember lying there, looking up at Orion while he was, you know, pumping and bucking or whatever, thinking, *Yes, this is right. This is all happening exactly as it should.*" Katie toggled through radio stations until she found a song she approved of. "He thought we were going to get married. Before I left for college, we were at Jimmy John's and he was all fidgety, barely touching his sub, and then all of a sudden he reached into the pocket of his windbreaker and presented me with a promise ring."

"Hold on," Cassidy interjected. "At the Jimmy John's?"

"At the Jimmy John's." Katie nodded. "He held out this ring to me in his thick, rough fingers with their chewed-down fingernails, but I wouldn't take it. I reminded him that I would be off to UT in the fall. And he said, 'That's why it's a promise.' So I said, 'I'm sorry, but I can't promise you any-thing.'"

"Heartbreaker," Cassidy said.

"He didn't take it well." Katie helped herself to a sip of coffee from Cassidy's travel mug in the truck's cup holder. "He stormed out of the restaurant and hurled the ring across the parking lot. He never spoke to me again after that."

Cassidy felt a sudden and unexpected empathy toward teenage Justin Barnes.

"So really you got proposed to twice." She reached over and tore a piece of Katie's bagel for herself. "Once at the Jimmy John's and a second time . . . I assume Paul Michael chose a more elaborate way to ask for your hand?"

"Are you kidding?" Katie said. "Paul Michael couldn't take a dump without being elaborate."

A nub of bagel lodged in Cassidy's throat. She washed it down with some coffee. "I hope you don't mean he proposed to you on the toilet."

"Worse," Katie said. "At a fancy brunch he put together. I preferred Justin's way, to be honest. At least it was sweet and sincere, true to who we were at the time."

Katie fiddled with the radio some more, switching from some soulful, aching song by Adele to something upbeat and twangy by Taylor Swift. "Paul Michael's proposal was all about exhibiting the fancy diamond ring he got me to all his friends. The whole thing was curated. It was . . . I don't even know how to put it."

"All for show?" Cassidy said.

Katie nodded. "I would have preferred for him to propose with a Ring Pop. Cherry because he actually cared enough to remember it's my favorite, you know?"

Cassidy kept her eyes on the road ahead.

"Paul Michael didn't get me," Katie said. "We didn't get

each other. I'm starting to think a lot of our relationship was just about . . ." She let her voice trickle off.

"Appearances?" Cassidy said.

Katie crumpled her bagel's white deli paper into a ball and tossed it into the plastic bag between her boots. "You know what? We're giving Paul Michael way too much airtime." She turned up the volume on the radio. "When we should be focusing on our song!"

Cassidy laughed. "We already have a song?"

"This is 'Our Song,'" Katie said over the blaring music. "By Taylor Swift. We can make it ours if you want to."

She leaned over and sang into Cassidy's ear, "'Cause our song is a slamming screen door, sneaking out late tapping on your window . . .'"

‑ঃ♡ঃ‑

Cassidy and Katie arrived at the ranch, a secluded stretch of wooded acreage and sinewy trails, around noon. Cassidy stepped down from the truck's running board, stretched her legs, and took it all in. Man, this place was rural. Gina wasn't kidding. There was a lot of dust here, and flies.

They trudged uphill to a log-cabin lodge where a hefty middle-aged woman sat behind the check-in desk, knitting a wool scarf. She looked up, bright eyed.

"Hi," Cassidy said, and the woman's expression altered in a way that Cassidy was all too familiar with. "We booked the private cabin. It's under the last name Price. First name Cassidy."

The woman set down her knitting. "ID," she said.

Cassidy handed it over.

Katie, perhaps sensing the tension, turned up her warmth. "This is such a beautiful place," she said. "Are you one of the owners?"

"I am," the woman said coldly. She placed a set of keys onto the counter. "Out the door to your left. It's a five-minute walk down the trail."

"Thank you." Cassidy took the keys and led Katie back outside. She could see the confusion on Katie's face, the dimmed light in her eyes, and it occurred to her that Katie had never been so quickly sized up and disliked before—by anyone.

They walked down to their cabin in silence. Cassidy unlocked and opened the door. "Rustic!" she said upon entering. "Mmm, what's that smell? Is that what hay smells like?"

"I don't think that woman liked us," Katie said.

Cassidy shut the door behind them. "She doesn't have to like us."

"Do you think she thought . . ."

"I don't know what she thought," Cassidy said. "But my guess is not a lot of people who look like me come around here. That's all."

"She assumed we were a couple, didn't she?" Katie said.

"Probably." Cassidy tried to sound consoling, but did Katie really not think that was likely to happen? What did she expect? "Don't let it ruin the weekend." Cassidy took a step closer to Katie. She wanted to put her arms around her but didn't.

"It won't." Katie walked over to the window and opened the blinds. "I don't know about you, but I'm ready to ride."

"I'm ready to watch you ride," Cassidy said.

Katie turned to her. "You're not leaving here without getting on a horse."

"Katie, the only horses I've come within a foot of have had police officers on top of them."

"Don't be a pussy," Katie said. "You're getting on a horse."

Cassidy wasn't one to abdicate control easily, and yet she soon found herself following Katie out to the stables, where they approached a white-haired man in a tweed flat cap. Thankfully his face was friendly.

"Hi there," Katie called out to him. "Are you Mr. Duncan?"

"Sure am." He wiped his palms on his Carhartt overalls before offering Katie his hand. "You can call me Buddy."

"Katie Daniels." Katie shook the old man's hand. "Pleased to meet you. I believe we spoke on the phone."

"Yes, that's right. You're the show-jumping champ."

"Wait, what?" Cassidy said.

"Got our Dutch Warmblood all ready for you," he said to

Katie. "Just like you asked." Then he turned to Cassidy. "And for you, sir?"

"Uh—" Cassidy stuttered. "This is my first time."

"Oh boy! All right. No jumper for you then."

"No, certainly not." Katie came to with a forced smile. "We'll both start with some nice and easy trail horses for now."

"All right then," Buddy said. "Will the mister need a lesson?"

"No," Cassidy answered for herself. "That's not necessary."

Katie's face had gone disturbingly red. "I'm an instructor," she said. "Used to be, I mean. Fully certified. I'll take care of he—m."

"Alrighty." Buddy shuffled into the stable.

Katie's cheeks, Cassidy noted, had not yet returned to their normal color. "Sorry," she said. "That happens sometimes. Are you freaked out?"

"It's fine." Katie pretended to adjust something on her boot.

Buddy reemerged then with two horses, one black, one brown.

"Zorro for you," he said to Katie. "And this here's Cocoa Puffs." He handed them each a helmet.

"Hold on." Cassidy squeezed her helmet onto her head and turned to Katie. "You get Zorro, and I get Cocoa Puffs?"

"Do you want Zorro?" Katie said.

"No, it's cool. Cocoa Puffs looks like a total stud."

"Actually, she's a mare." Katie showed Cassidy how to take the reins and guide her horse toward the trail.

"Nice to give me the heads-up that you're some riding champion or whatever," Cassidy said.

"Back home we're a dime a dozen," Katie said. "And that was a long time ago."

"Were you bullshitting him about being an instructor?"

Katie shook her head. "I taught for a few years, summers during high school."

"You're just full of surprises, aren't you?"

They walked till there were no other people around and no sounds but the wind in the trees and whinnies in the distance.

"Okay," Katie said. "Ready for your lesson?"

"You really expect me to get on this thing?" Cassidy eyed her horse from nose to tail. "Can't we just keep walking them like this, like big dogs?"

"Lesson one," Katie said. "Getting on. I want you to stick your left toe in the stirrup, and put your right hand on the back of the saddle to hoist yourself up. Then swing your right leg over the horse's back. Once you have one leg on either side of her, sit down gently and put your other foot in the other stirrup."

Cassidy did exactly as she was told, proud of succeeding on her first try, then immediately sorry. "Holy shit this is high up. I don't like this. I'm going to fall."

"You're not going to fall," Katie said, but she seemed poised and ready to catch Cassidy if she did. "Be confident or she'll sense your fear, and when horses get scared they run."

"Fantastic."

Katie took a few steps back. "Now you're going to make the horse walk."

"Do I have to?" Cassidy gripped too tight to the reins.

"You have to relax," Katie said. "And move with the horse. Sit up tall, shoulders squared, heels down in the stirrups. Keep your eyes focused ahead of you between Cocoa Puffs's ears."

"I think you can just call her Cocoa for short, honestly."

"Use the reins to steer," Katie continued. "Move the left rein left or the right rein right, in a motion like you're opening a door. To slow down or stop, pull back gently. Got it?"

Cassidy stayed very still. "I think so."

"Good." In one swift motion Katie was up on her horse. "Let's walk together," she said. "Follow me. To get her to move, hug your legs around her, and rock forward in the saddle."

Cassidy did as Katie said, and to her amazement Cocoa Puffs began taking steps forward, following just behind Zorro. The horse seemed to know what to do, so Cassidy tried to do as little as possible. In a few minutes, she calmed down enough to recognize how beautiful this was. The landscape. The day. Katie.

"This isn't so bad," she said.

Katie steered Zorro around so the two of them could continue along side by side. "Want to go a little faster?"

"Okay."

"Listen first," Katie said. "To tell Cocoa you want her to go from a walk to a trot, you need to gently squeeze her sides with the insides of your legs. If that doesn't work, you might need to give her a gentle kick. But sit deeply, press your legs down, and keep your back tall and straight, otherwise—"

Cassidy did as she was told, forgetting the part about listening first, and the horse was off.

"Whoa," Cassidy yelled. "Whoa! Stop!" She yanked at the reins, but that only made the horse run faster. "Heel! Heel! Stop running!"

Suddenly they were up on two legs, the horse's two hind legs, and Cassidy was flying backward through midair.

She landed hard on the ground, while her horse galloped full speed ahead into the distance.

When she opened her eyes, she saw blue sky, then Katie bent over her. "Oh my god. Are you okay? Are you hurt?"

Cassidy lifted her head, made sure she could move her arms, her legs. "I'm fine. I'm—aah. I just pulled a muscle trying to break my fall."

"I should have told you to never try to break your fall," Katie said.

"Yeah, thanks for that."

Katie assessed Cassidy's body for injuries, checked for damage to her helmet. "I'm sorry I made you do this."

"No, this is great. I'm having a great time."

"Let's go back to the cabin," Katie said.

Cassidy sat up slowly. "What about Cocoa Puffs?"

"I'll have Buddy go get her."

In the safety of their cabin, Cassidy and Katie could finally break down and laugh.

"You flew up in the air so high." Katie uncorked the bottle of wine they'd brought from home. "I saw it happening in slow motion."

"It sure wasn't happening in slow motion for me." Cassidy rubbed at her throbbing shoulder. "It was like I blinked my eyes and the next thing I knew I had dirt in my mouth."

"I told you to sit deeply and press your legs down." Katie brought Cassidy her glass in bed.

"Oh fuck off," Cassidy said.

"Are you sure you're okay?"

"I'm fine. Just humiliated."

"At least let me massage your shoulder for you." Katie set down her wineglass on the end table and climbed behind Cassidy. She kneaded her thumbs into Cassidy's tender muscles. "How's that?" she asked.

"That's very good." Cassidy closed her eyes and tried to relax.

"Can I ask you something?"

"You can ask me anything. Except to get back onto a horse ever again."

Katie's hands came to rest on Cassidy's shoulders. "Why didn't you correct Buddy before? When he called you 'sir'?"

Cassidy reopened her eyes and turned around. She adjusted herself on the bed so that she and Katie were face-to-face. "Sometimes it's just not worth the trouble."

"Does it bother you?" Katie asked. "When people call you 'sir'?"

"Not really. Does it bother you?"

Katie fidgeted with the hem of the plaid bedspread. "Do you wish you were a man?"

"Would you rather I were a man?"

"I don't know," Katie said.

Cassidy tried not to flinch. "I appreciate your honesty."

"I didn't mean that to sound . . ."

"No, I'm serious," Cassidy said. "I want you to be honest with me."

"This is me being honest." Katie leaned in and kissed Cassidy gently on the lips. "The rest is me trying to understand."

Katie was a portrait of coziness in her outdoorsy attire,

framed by the knotty pine walls, but Cassidy could see she was struggling. "Are you trying to understand me?" Cassidy asked. "Or you?"

"I want to understand us," Katie said. "But I also just want us to take our clothes off right now and not think about any of it."

"I want that, too." Cassidy reached for Katie's flannel and drew her in.

They should talk about this. Of course they should talk about this.

She undid Katie's top button.

Katie complied by reaching under Cassidy's shirt. She ran her fingers across Cassidy's taut stomach. "You know how you felt out there on the ranch?" she said. "Like you were out of your element?"

A trail of goose bumps followed the path of Katie's fingertips upon Cassidy's skin.

"That's how I feel with you." She traced her way down to Cassidy's hipbones. "I don't know how to touch you." She glided her fingertips down the inside of Cassidy's thigh. "But I want to."

Cassidy kissed Katie's neck, took her earlobe into her mouth. She whispered into Katie's ear, "I'll show you."

SEVENTEEN

There was no polite way of putting it. Cassidy had fucked Katie's brains out. Katie's brains were lost in the mess of sheets or somewhere on the cabin floor, while the rest of her continued lying there, naked and spent, flat upon her back.

"I didn't know my body could even do whatever that was," she said.

Cassidy sat propped up beside her, her long legs crossed at the ankles. "That last time?"

"No, the second time. Where were you even? It felt like you were in me up to your elbow."

"Not quite." Cassidy chuckled.

"And then that last time." Katie sat up, closed her eyes for a moment to reimagine it—how she had her hand full of Cassidy and Cassidy had her hand full of her, and she hadn't thought she could come again since she'd already broken her all-time record with that second time, but then she felt it approaching, and Cassidy said, "Slow down, stay with me."

Which was code, Katie realized, for *Don't come yet.*

Katie had never tried to keep an orgasm at bay before. Usually it was a fight to get one to happen, so her first thought was, Nah, I'm gonna go with this, but you do you.

"Stay with me," Cassidy said, and her eyes told Katie she had to at least try, so Katie did, and their bodies took on a rhythm, like the kind you think of when you think of sex, but Katie felt it this time, for real.

"Don't hold your breath," Cassidy said. "Breathe with me." So Katie did, and it was a slow build of wave upon wave, "Stay with me, stay with me," until the two of them together—

"I've never actually come at the same time as anyone before," Katie said. "I thought that was just something girls pretended could happen to get the guy to finish."

Cassidy blinked her eyes at Katie a few times but remained silent.

"Did you feel what I felt when that happened?" Katie asked.

"Of course I did." Cassidy took Katie's hand in hers and rested it upon her own heart. "Do you feel what I feel right now? For you?"

Katie pulled her hand away. "I'm sorry. Heartbeats freak me out. I don't like the idea of this force pump inside us having to work so hard all the time to keep us alive."

"Romantic," Cassidy said.

"I do feel it, though," Katie said. "I feel the romance."

"Does it scare you more or less than having a beating heart?" Cassidy asked.

"Honestly?" Katie shook out the rumpled bedspread in search of her undergarments. "I thought this weekend was going to be about us becoming better friends, that you were going to say what happened between us last week was just a onetime thing, something we had to get out of the way."

"And now?"

Katie located her underwear and slid them on. "Did you ever have girlfriends growing up? I mean, friends who were girls, who you were totally obsessed with? And it seemed like no matter how much time you spent together it was never enough?" Katie grabbed Cassidy's chambray button-down from the floor and put it on. "You know that high-strung, excitable bond that a girl could only really have with her best girlfriend?"

"Yeah," Cassidy said. "I've had that."

"What happens when all of that gets rolled up into the same person you're sleeping with?"

"So you're obsessed with me," Cassidy said.

"I think so." Katie let herself laugh. "Like schoolgirl, batshit-crazy obsessed."

"See?" Cassidy reached out to rest her hand on Katie's heart. "You do feel what I feel for you."

On the drive back into the city Katie's cell phone rang.

She had to rummage all the way to the bottom of her purse to find it—that's how much time had passed since she'd last checked for messages, enough that her Kleenex soft pack and travel-size Aveeno had overtaken her phone in the purse hierarchy.

"Good lord. It's my mother. I didn't return her last call, and she's been really nervous since I've been living alone again."

Cassidy switched off the radio. "Pick it up."

Katie pressed *answer* and turned toward the passenger-side window. "Hey, Mama. I can't really talk. I'm driving in a car."

"Where are you, Katie?" Her mother's tone was, as usual, equal parts suspicion and anxiety. "You didn't return my call from yesterday."

"I'm just heading back into the city from upstate." Katie made her voice extra upbeat. "A friend and I went riding."

"In New York you went riding?"

"That's right," Katie said, hearing her own overzealous

twang sneaking its way back into her diction. "It's like farm country up there. But I'm going to call you later once I'm back home tonight, okay?"

"Who are you with?" her mother asked.

"Just a friend," Katie said. "No one you know."

"I haven't gotten a letter from you all month and now you're not answering my calls. How do you expect me not to worry?"

"I know and I'm sorry, but with everything that's been going on—"

"Every day I go to the mailbox."

"I know, Mama. I'm sorry. But you're breaking up something terrible, I can barely hear you, so I'll call you later when I'm home, okay? Bye now." Katie ended the call and turned her phone screen-side-down on her lap.

Cassidy kept her eyes on the road ahead.

"Sorry," Katie said.

"For what?"

Katie wasn't entirely sure. "I shouldn't have answered."

"Of course you should have," Cassidy said, like all was good, but the euphoria they'd been enjoying had come to a crashing halt.

Katie had the sudden urge to throw open the truck door and run—similar to how she'd run off after going home with that random guy she met online, when she found herself in a puddle of her own tears at an abandoned construction site, when she called Cassidy that first time. When this whole thing really got started.

"You okay?" Cassidy asked.

"Yeah." Katie shoved her cell phone back into her bag. "My mom just gets to me sometimes."

Cassidy nodded. "That's what mothers do."

Katie reached for the water bottle rolling around at her feet, opened it, and drank. She tried to imagine, just for a minute, what it would be like to take Cassidy home to meet her family. Instead she recalled the first time she brought home Paul Michael—how hard she'd worked to prepare her family beforehand for Paul Michael's erudition, the way he wore only black or gray, his habit of interrupting others. How he didn't eat animals or anything that came from an animal, and that this was called vegan. She'd worked equally hard to prepare Paul Michael for her grandmother's saltiness and her mother's mistrust of outsiders, her father's rugged pride in being a "straight shooter" and her brothers' tendency to be outright gross.

Katie remembered how she felt when they pulled up to the modest brick house she'd grown up in, how she took comfort in its impeccably manicured lawn and welcoming front porch. She knocked on the familiar screen door, confident that she'd laid the proper foundation for all parties—that everyone would play nice and be respectful. After all, her family and Paul Michael shared one major thing in common, and that was Katie.

Didn't they all want to see her happy?

And yet the moment her father pointed a forkful of pulled pork at Paul Michael over the dinner table, Katie knew it was hopeless. "So it's not that you can't eat this," her father said. "It's that you won't."

Her grandmother lit a fresh cigarette with the butt of her spent one. "What are you, Gandhi on a hunger strike?"

Her mother ignored Paul Michael for the entire visit, and consistently for the next four years. She waited until Katie called home to announce their engagement to finally speak up. "I just don't know about this boy, Katie. He makes me uncomfortable."

"I love him," Katie had said. "And I trust him. He can give me a good stable life, and he isn't one to stray."

Katie had highlighted those aspects of Paul Michael's character because she knew they would speak directly to her mother's fears, but also because they were true—Katie was sure of it. But her mother had turned out to be right about Paul Michael, hadn't she? What if Katie had simply listened to her mother from the start? How much heartache and wasted time could have been saved?

"Do you want to tell me what's going on in your head right now?" Cassidy asked. "Did your mother say something to upset you?"

Katie loved her family. Her parents were decent, whole-hearted people. They just weren't the best about others who were different from them. How could Katie express that to Cassidy without her misunderstanding it as a personal attack? How could she put into words that even now, after years of living in New York and evolving into a fully capable independent woman, she still struggled with where her parents' beliefs ended and hers began?

"I'm fine." Katie switched the radio back on. "Just tired."

Cassidy tilted her head at Katie in a way that indicated she knew she was lying. Her dark sunglasses shielded the eye roll that Katie was certain accompanied the motion.

Katie already knew Cassidy well enough to understand her every tick and gesture for what it really meant. How she scratched the back of her head when she was nervous, snickered when she felt threatened, touched her lips when she was lost in thought. How her eyes got big and round when she let her guard down, and how she blushed when she was caught being kind.

The head tilt/eye roll combo meant Cassidy was disappointed in Katie's failure to speak her mind but that she would let it go—and Katie was fine with that.

"Let's talk about something else," Katie said. "What's going on with the Met getting shut down?"

Cassidy thought for a minute. "Nothing's going on with it; it just is."

"Are you freaking out?" Katie asked.

"What's there to freak out over?" Cassidy kept her eyes on the road ahead. "Places close all the time."

"But you must be sad. Isn't that bar like your Cheers?"

Cassidy let out a laugh. "It's where I learned to be gay. I've been going there since I was nineteen, on a fake ID everyone knew was fake."

"It was the very first bathroom you had sex in . . . ," Katie said, only half joking.

"Actually no." Cassidy smirked. "But probably the second."

"I guess I set myself up for that one." Katie unscrewed the cap on her water bottle and took a sip. "What do you mean it's where you learned to be gay?"

"Why, you interested in getting lessons?"

"Fuck off," Katie said.

"I'm just playing." Cassidy tapped the top of Katie's knee and then got quiet for a second. She stared straight ahead, trying to give Katie a real answer to her question. "I guess going there as an awkward kid and getting hit on, like, almost immediately upon stepping foot in the door. It was kind of life altering."

A hint of astonishment came into Cassidy's voice, but her eyes remained unmoved. "I guess it struck me," she said, "that I might not fit quite right into the world at large, but in this filthy little bar I was something. I was considered hot. I had power."

Katie got the feeling Cassidy hadn't let this all properly sink in till right now. "So you must be upset about it closing," she said. "Even I'm kind of sad about it and I've only been there a couple of times."

Cassidy shrugged.

"Is there anything we can do?" Katie wouldn't be deterred. "Have you looked into the nature of the sale? Is it still pending? Did you check with the register's office?"

Cassidy turned to look at Katie straight on then. She held her gaze for a split second longer than was comfortable considering she was driving a vehicle. "I appreciate your solidarity," she said. "But yes, I did all those things. And it's a lost cause."

Katie felt herself deflate in a way that she wasn't sure she was entitled to. This was Cassidy's loss, not hers. The Met didn't belong to her the way it belonged to Cassidy and her friends.

And yet, the way Cassidy described her first time entering the bar, how life altering it was—that was kind of what had happened to Katie, too. She remembered how her initial fear of the place had quickly dissolved into a sense of comfort and camaraderie that she had never experienced in a bar before. So maybe Katie belonged more than she thought.

Either way, she was taking it personally—how the Met had come to her and was now being taken away. Whether or not she'd earned her membership, Katie wanted to keep going back, and she would miss the place as her own.

Just then, some renegade SUV cut them off and Cassidy palmed the horn. Her attention was diverted to bypassing some slow-moving traffic ahead. She weaved their rented pickup around elderly Buicks and wavering Toyotas, impatient, confident, tailgating up to the very edge of obnoxious.

"Sometimes I think you're more boy than any boy I've ever dated," Katie said.

Cassidy smirked. "I'm going to choose to take that as a compliment."

EIGHTEEN

Cassidy clicked buy and waited for her confirmation number to appear on-screen. She wasn't ballsy enough to make this online purchase using her work computer, so she had her personal laptop out on her desk.

In the days since her and Katie's trip to the ranch they had spent most of their time together indoors, either in bed or on the couch. On the floor or the kitchen table. A few times in the shower.

In the middle of last week, Cassidy had even snuck out of work early—which she had never done before under any circumstances. Usually she was among the first to arrive in the morning, already neck-deep in documents at her desk while her associates, junior and senior, filed in. Hours later she'd watch them file out, texting on their way to the elevators, while she remained at her desk. She knew all the night-shift cleaners by name. Sometimes they'd ask about her life as she dumped the contents of her own trash can into the bin. With no kids, no spouse, not much in the way of personal responsibility, she was often at a loss as to what to tell them.

"I like to work hard," she'd say.

She didn't tell them that this was her edge—her single-minded focus, no one and nothing else slowing her down, that it was her guarantee of making partner, maybe before she turned forty. In her five years with the firm, Cassidy had stayed at work with fevers, toothaches, even food poisoning. The time her father had a heart attack scare, she'd headed to the hospital only after she sent her last round of comments to her client.

But there she'd been on a random, nothing-special night in the middle of last week plotting an early escape from her desk. The weather outside was perfect—she knew because she'd checked the weather app on her phone. It was an ideal night for a long walk on the High Line, followed by dinner nearby at Santina or Cookshop or anyplace with a cluster of outdoor tables.

She texted Katie. *It's beautiful outside. Let's make the most of it. Can you sneak out early?*

Katie wrote back, *How early?*

Now?

Now?? It's not even 7.

This was the problem with Katie's being a fellow workaholic. She could be even more of a challenge to persuade than Cassidy herself.

The sun's about to set, Cassidy wrote. *Meet me at the High Line. I'll make it worth your while.*

Katie didn't write back immediately—a hopeful sign. She was considering it.

A full two minutes went by before Cassidy received her reply: *You're becoming a terrible influence.*

Ha. She had her.

Cassidy jumped to standing and pushed in her chair, then pulled her chair back out. She decided to leave her briefcase wide open on the floor and her overcoat hanging on its hanger. It was worth being chilly in order to leave the appearance that she'd stepped away for only a moment.

She tried to look busy as she fled from her office, down the hall, and around the corner—where she bumped right into Hamlin. Of course. Who else would be lurking about the elevators like an insect spy drone?

He stood back and stuck his thumbs into his suspenders. "Already heading out?"

"No. No." Cassidy pushed past him. She would not be deterred. "Just for a second. I'll be right back."

She cursed his name all the way downtown but forgot he existed the instant she found Katie waiting for her on the corner of Twenty-Third Street and Tenth Avenue. They ascended the stairs to the repurposed rail line side by side, two dark suits in a narrow parade of jeans and sneakers.

When they reached a stretch of green lawn Katie took off her heels and carried them at her side, hooked from her fingers. In bare feet she was three inches shorter than Cassidy, which for some reason only made it harder for Cassidy to not reach for her, draw her in, wrap her arms around her.

They missed the sunset, but the sky had turned an electric blue that set everything aglow. As they continued along a winding sweet-scented path of shrubs and trees, the light deepened and they soon found themselves alone, secluded in what felt like a magical forest.

Katie stopped and turned to Cassidy. Her eyes were bright with twilight, and Cassidy could feel the pull of her.

How did this happen? This impossible, hysterical, hopeless need.

Cassidy could almost see them from above, watching herself from the moon or an overhead branch as she leaned in, slowly.

"Let's go to your place," Katie said.

Cassidy came to a halt, shaken from the moment. "What about dinner?"

"Let's go to your place," Katie said again.

So they were off, rushing through the night, back through

the teeming city streets, through the entrance to Cassidy's building and across its watchful lobby, past Frank, then up and into her apartment, door slamming behind them—where finally, at last, they could press together and fuse into one.

The rest of the week Cassidy was a no-show at Metropolis, dodging texts from Gina. *Where are u? Stop being avoidant. You can't pretend this bar isn't closing!!!*

Over the weekend, she and Katie gave up on leaving the apartment altogether. Monday morning arrived and it occurred to Cassidy that she hadn't worn shoes since Friday.

Which was why here, now, seated at her work desk with her laptop open before her, Cassidy felt the need for a grand gesture. She wanted to take Katie somewhere special that not only required shoes but also was an event—an experience that would create a new shared memory.

This gala at the Metropolitan Opera House seemed like just the thing.

Ticket purchase confirmed, Cassidy shut her laptop and slid it into her briefcase. She could breathe again, ready now to return her undivided attention to her work.

NINETEEN

The moment Katie settled into Vivienne's salon chair and was covered in that familiar black cape, she felt safe in the way she imagined some people must feel at their therapist's office. But Vivienne had to be better than any psychoanalyst. She was wise beyond her twenty-six years, wild enough to never be judgmental, and the lazy d's and dropped r's of her southern Louisiana drawl always put Katie at ease. Katie felt silly for putting off this haircut for so long out of fear.

Today Vivienne's hair was brown, parted in the middle, and fell past her shoulders in beachy waves. It was different every time Katie saw her, and she seemed to never repeat the same look twice, which was an antsy creativity she also applied to her dating life. Katie had been living vicariously through Vivienne's storied adventures for years.

"Same as usual?" Vivienne swung Katie's chair around so she was facing herself in the mirror.

No, Katie wanted to say, *everything is different.* But Vivienne didn't wait for an answer to begin Katie's usual cut.

"So how are the wedding plans coming along?" she asked.

Katie let the question hang in the air for a few seconds. She had sat like this and talked to Vivienne every six weeks for the past five years—which made her, to date, Katie's most lasting and consistent relationship—but she had yet to ever match the shock value of one of Vivienne's scandal-ridden stories with her own.

"We broke up," Katie said. After all the anxiety leading to this moment, Katie was surprised by how the words left her mouth now like an easy breath.

Vivienne laughed.

"I'm totally serious."

Vivienne's comb went still. She studied Katie's face in the mirror. "Oh my goodness, you're not joking." Her scissors came down at her side. "Are you okay?"

Katie nodded. "I'm great, actually."

Vivienne brought her usually untamed voice down to a Southern-comfort whisper. "Was it another man?"

"Another woman," Katie said.

"He cheated on you," Vivienne said, some of the spice returning to her speech, "and you're this together right now? I knew you had some bounce to you, Katie, but sweet baby Jesus."

"It's kind of funny," Katie said. "I don't really miss him. I mean, I thought I'd miss him more than I do. Instead I feel like I'm learning what I like to do now."

Vivienne's comb and scissors returned to their task. She was working on automatic, temporarily dumbfounded.

"Like if I never go to another art opening for as long as I live," Katie said, "where I have to listen to some dude talk nonsense about how his arrangement of a bunch of mirrors is a Borgesian statement on perception, it'll be too soon, you know?"

Vivienne politely nodded.

Katie wanted to tell her more. She wanted to tell Vivienne everything. From her and Cassidy's crazy first meeting, to their fast friendship, to their kiss, to their weekend getaway—right up to the past ten days of sexual bliss. Just running it through her mind, Katie could hardly believe how close she and Cassidy had gotten, how inseparable they'd become in such a short amount of time. How they were maybe falling in love. Katie wanted to try out the words.

"Well good for you." Vivienne seemed to click back into place. "Best thing now," she said, "is to not get involved with anyone else for a while. Take some time, have some fun. Whatever you do, don't jump back into a relationship right away."

Katie watched the split ends of her hair fall from her head to the floor. "Yeah," she said. "You're probably right."

Vivienne snipped, combed, snipped.

"So tell me about *your* latest dating adventure," Katie said.

Vivienne went on to regale Katie with her latest escapade with an acupuncturist who picked her up using the line *I can't wait to get my needles into you.*

"He's a little freaky," Vivienne told her. "But my lower-back pain has never felt better."

By the time Katie stepped out of the salon freshly cut and styled, she was convinced there was little an hour with Vivienne couldn't make better. She was also newly certain of how impossible Vivienne's casual attitude toward dating would be for her. If taking some time to have fun, not getting involved with anyone too seriously too soon, required a willingness to be some weirdo's sexual pincushion, well, forget it.

Katie walked west till she hit Sixth Avenue, where the street was closed for a food festival. Tents and tables displaying everything from dinosaur-size turkey legs to handmade ice-cream sandwiches lined both sides of the sidewalk. Cassidy was supposed to come over later with takeout, but Katie couldn't resist trying a free sample or two before heading home.

Katie scanned the offerings, homed in on a vendor giving

out Dixie cups of artisanal beef jerky, and was making her way over when she caught sight of a familiar-looking shark-fin fauxhawk alongside a purple do-rag. It was Gina and Becky.

Katie's first instinct was to turn the other way and bolt, but what if they saw her seeing them? She couldn't chance such a rude gesture, so instead she urged herself to continue forward.

"Hey there," she said, once she was just beside them.

"Well hello." Becky smacked Gina on the shoulder. "What are you doing here?"

"Just passing through," Katie said. "You?"

"Our friend has a booth." Becky nodded toward a table where a woman with asymmetrical bangs and tattooed fore-arms, whom Katie could have sworn she'd met before, was slinging fried fish cakes shaped like baseballs.

"You should check it out," Becky said. "Best fritters you'll find outside the Caribbean. Ask for the special sauce if you think you can handle spice."

Katie smiled. "I can handle spice." Before she found her-self challenging Becky to a hot-sauce-eating contest, Katie looked to Gina, who was scarfing down some kind of meat on a stick. "Looks tasty," Katie said.

"You can't have a bite," Gina mumbled back.

"That's okay, I'm good." Katie glanced left, then right, to

decipher her most efficient escape route. "Well, it was nice running into y'all," she said. "But I better get—"

"Not so fast." Becky caught Katie by the wrist. "While we have you here . . . I would be remiss if I didn't mention that we've noticed you and Cassidy have been spending a lot of time together."

Katie rechecked her getaway paths. "Uh-huh," she said.

"So . . ." Becky toggled her head from side to side.

"So what's up with that?" Gina said.

Katie could feel her ears beneath her fresh blowout getting hot. "I'm not sure I understand."

"I guess we've just been curious," Becky said, "about your intentions. The thing is, we haven't seen much of Cassidy lately, and we're worried she's not really processing everything going on, with the bar closing and all . . ."

"Cassidy's putting all her eggs in the Katie basket right now is what we're saying," Gina interjected, mouth full of meat.

"Cassidy's uncharacteristically vulnerable right now," Becky continued. "Even though it may not look like it from the outside. So if you're not . . ."

"If you're just playing with her," Gina said, "now's not the time. Have you ever even do-si-doed with a girl before?"

Katie did a double take. "Excuse me?"

"Allow me to translate." Becky put up her hands in the little shark's defense. "What Gina means is, are you even gay?"

"I don't know," Katie said. "What difference does that make?"

Gina coughed, nearly choking herself with her meat stick.

"Hey, that's cool," Becky said. "Nobody here has a problem with that."

"I do." Gina pounded her chest till she stopped coughing. "You should know," she said to Katie. And then to Becky, "She should know."

Katie had had just about enough of this. "Look, I appreciate that you're looking out for your friend," she said. "I admire that, I really do. Loyal friends aren't easy to come by; trust me, I know this firsthand. But if you'll excuse me—"

"It's a simple question." Gina cut her off. "Do you like girls? Is. That. A. Thing. You. Do?"

"I don't know if I like girls," Katie shot back. "But I like Cassidy. And you should be ashamed of yourself for passing judgment on me. You of all people should be wary of trying to put people in boxes. My feelings for Cassidy are real, and you're right, we've been spending a lot of time together, mostly in bed doing the four-legged foxtrot, not that it's any of your damn business."

Gina swallowed down a last bite of meat, licked her lips, and tossed her empty stick to the ground. "Okay," she said to Becky. "She's growing on me."

TWENTY

When the reminder popped up on Cassidy's calendar for that evening's appointment with Gerard, she could hardly believe three months had already gone by. Last time she saw him, she'd just gotten out of that misguided, short-lived affair with Hot Sarah from hot yoga, but here it was already time to get fitted for next season's shirts and suits and jackets, and Katie was a name that Cassidy could no longer utter without smiling—and Gerard had yet to hear of her.

How had so much happened in so little time? It made Cassidy wonder if things with Katie were moving too fast.

Cassidy sent off one final email before heading out. Then, briefcase in hand, she continued worrying along Seventh Avenue.

Had she been too hasty buying those tickets to the Met

Opera gala? Her sudden lack of confidence on the matter felt like more than simple buyer's remorse. It was stress. Anxiety.

When was the last time Cassidy had felt anxious about a girl? When she was eighteen? How the hell was she supposed to know if this kind of fancy date was too much too soon? She never dated. She didn't woo girls, or bow and twist into new shapes to get someone to like her back.

Cassidy checked her watch, then her phone, then her reflection in a passing storefront window.

Caring too much made a person weak. It opened you up to all sorts of vulnerabilities, and it was making Cassidy do ridiculous things—spending hours online searching for the perfect night out, envisioning Katie and herself together in extravagant clothes surrounded by fairy-tale glamour like something from a storybook. As if anything so conventional and ceremonious, such normalized enchantment, could ever be hers.

She could give the tickets away or forget about them altogether. No one would ever have to know she'd been drawn to spend her hard-earned money on anything so queasily romantic. But just the idea of doing that almost took her breath away.

Cassidy checked her watch again, to see she'd arrived only six minutes late. Not bad. She swung open the tall glass door and entered with confidence in her step.

The elevator operator, a mustachioed young man in a houndstooth waistcoat, greeted her and escorted her upward. A moment later he unfolded the vintage lift's scissor gate and Cassidy stepped through to where Gerard was waiting.

"Hello, hello." A cheek kiss left, a cheek kiss right. As always, Gerard was dressed in a flamboyant mix of patterns and jewel tones only a dandy with a stylist's courage could get away with. It helped that he was a beautiful mix of Puerto Rican and Greek, which he proudly referred to as Puerto Greekan.

"How are you, my favorite? I've set out a selection of new fabrics for you." He led Cassidy to a long table covered in a mosaic of cloth swatches. "Shirts here. Suits and jackets there. But first, you must tell me the latest gossip from the lipstick jungle. I heard your beloved Metropolis is not long for this world."

"That is true." Cassidy approached a faceless, fully dressed mannequin.

Gerard followed after her. "It's absolutely heartbreaking, isn't it? To lose a place like that after all these years."

"What's this sport coat?" Cassidy asked. "It's really soft."

"Honey." Gerard stood still. "Aren't you the least bit upset? I assumed that bar was where they'd sprinkle your ashes after you died."

"I guess they'll have to come up with a new plan for my ashes," Cassidy said.

"So tough, aren't you. Never let them see you sweat." Gerard shook his head. "That's a new arrival," he said, indicating the sport coat Cassidy was interested in. "It's a blend of cashmere and vicuna, but it's unstructured, only half lined. This is a much more casual, relaxed fit than you usually go for."

"I like it," Cassidy said. "I'll give it a try."

"Well aren't you surprising today?" Gerard stripped the jacket from the mannequin. "Just when you think you know a person's inner-layer preference, they throw all caution to the wind."

"That's sort of been my mood lately, I guess." Cassidy returned to the shirt swatches.

Gerard picked up one that was a shade of pale blue. "You'll probably like this. It's similar to the broadcloth you usually get, but with a higher thread count, giving it a slightly smoother, silkier feel."

Cassidy felt the swatch between her thumb and forefinger. "That's nice." She reached across the table to the far corner for a pin-dotted swatch. "This is kind of fun and different."

"A pattern?" Gerard was taken aback. "What's gotten into you?" He narrowed his eyes, looked Cassidy up and down. "You seem lighter."

"You think I lost weight?"

"Lighter like brighter," he said. "Happier. In spite of the

fact that the center of your world is about to be jackham-
mered to bits."

Cassidy smiled. "I think I'm in love." The words came
spilling out of her mouth before she could stop them, but
what safer space did she have to try out these words? Gerard
was the greatest lover of love she'd ever known.

He gasped, then brought the back of his hand to his forehead and pretended to pass out onto the table of fabrics.

"Okay," Cassidy said. "That's quite enough."

"Forgive me." He returned to standing and began fan-
ning himself. "I never thought I'd see the day."

"Me neither," Cassidy said. "Believe me. But this girl is
special."

"Are you talking"—Gerard brought his voice down to a
conspiratorial whisper— "monogamy?"

Cassidy nodded. "Maybe . . . ?"

"Are you capable of that?"

"I guess we're going to find out," Cassidy said.

"Tears. I'm weeping tears of joy." Gerard whisked a silk
handkerchief from his breast pocket and dabbed at the
corner of his eye.

If only everyone in Cassidy's life could be so encourag-
ing. Although Gerard was a rare and special believer in
happy endings. He'd married his so-called high school
sweetheart, a boy who'd savagely bullied him throughout
adolescence until he kissed him senior year while drunk on a

post-pep-rally bottle of Boone's. They'd been together now for eighteen fairy-tale years.

"Who is this spell-casting girl?" Gerard asked. "Do you have a picture?"

"I do." Cassidy reached into her pocket for her phone. "It's not the best photo, though. She was sleeping when I took it."

"You photographed her while she slept?" Gerard covered his mouth with his hands. "This *is* serious."

He dashed to a shelf of fabric binders and pulled one down. "You have to let me design your wedding tux. We'll do a purple paisley just like the one I wore."

"Don't push your luck," Cassidy said.

TWENTY-ONE

....

Katie had been crouched over her living room table struggling to compose this letter since she'd arrived home from her haircut more than an hour ago. The dodging of her mother's phone calls and lying by omission had to stop. If she didn't give the woman something of substance to chew on soon, Minnie Daniels just might hire a bounty hunter to drag Katie home.

The wooden stationery box her mother had bought her sat on the couch beside Katie with its lid open, flaunting its neat compartments, everything in its rightful place. Paper in the center section. Pens on the left. Envelopes and stamps to the right. All with the geometric command of a divided lunch tray.

Katie had never expected to enjoy writing letters home or for the ritual itself to be soothing, but over the years she'd come to look forward to the ceremony of it, like a fortnightly meditation.

Sometimes it was easier than talking to her mother on the phone.

But not tonight.

Katie tapped the back of her roller-ball pen on yet another blank sheet of ecru monogrammed paper. Numerous failed attempts lay in crumpled balls at her feet.

She began again.

Dear Mama, I'm sorry it's been a while since my last letter. It hasn't been for lack of trying. In fact I've sat down a few times now to put my thoughts into words these past few weeks, and each time I've failed.

Katie thought for a second, probing her mind for the right words now.

Something's happened. I've met someone.

No.

I have news. I've met someone!

No.

I've made a new friend, Katie wrote. *A wonderful friend.*

I thought my life was over when Paul Michael betrayed me, but I'm beginning to realize . . . that I might be . . .

Nope. Katie crumpled the page into a ball and tossed it

onto the floor with the others. Her mother would throw a proper Southern fit if she knew how much of this fancy bond paper was going into the trash.

Okay. Here we go.

> *Dear Mama,*
>
> *I'm sorry it's been a while since my last letter. I know you've been worried about me since Paul Michael left, but I'm happy to report that I feel more alive than I have in years.*
>
> *You were right all along, Mama. He wasn't right for me. He never was.*
>
> *Like you suggested, I've tried to go out and socialize and make some new friends. I've met some truly interesting new people.*

Katie paused.

I've even gone on a few dates?

No.

I went on one date . . . with a handsome man named Jeremy. He had excellent manners and . . .

Katie crossed out *and* with a single strikethrough.

. . . but I don't think I'll see him again.

Perhaps I need more time before seeking out love or romance. It might be better to take things slowly and remember how to be alone. In the meantime, I'm very much hoping to cultivate new female friendships. What do you always say? Friends are God's way of apologizing to us for our families? Haha.

A knock at Katie's door caused her to startle. She put her pen down onto her letter and went to the peephole.

"It's me," Cassidy said. "The downstairs door was open."

"You're early." Katie unbolted the lock.

"Only by a half hour." Cassidy stepped inside with a takeout bag in one hand and her briefcase in the other. "I picked up Dig Inn."

Katie glanced at the clock and realized just how long she'd been sitting there trying to compose her letter.

Cassidy dropped her briefcase at the door and headed toward the living room to set down the food on the table. "Whoa, what's all this?"

"Nothing." Katie lunged for her letter in progress. She swept it up before Cassidy could get a look at it and folded it in half.

Cassidy raised an eyebrow. "Do you have a secret pen pal?"

"My mom."

"You write your mom letters in longhand?" Cassidy placed the takeout bag down onto the floor. "Is she Amish?"

"She thinks email is too impersonal." Katie picked up each of the crumpled rejects from the floor, gathered them together into one tight ecru paper ball, and stuffed it into her stationery box.

"I like your little setup here." Cassidy slid her fingers

along the edge of the wooden box. "It's like a bento box, but with writing materials instead of sushi. Is that an embossing stamp?"

"My mother gave me the box when I moved to New York." Katie slammed its lid shut and latched it. "The stationery is my Christmas gift every year."

"Your mom gives you the paper she wants you to write her letters on?" Cassidy cracked a smile.

"Uh-huh," Katie said.

"And I thought my mother was controlling."

"Watch it." Katie held up her pen like a knife. "Or I'll stab you with my quill."

Cassidy nodded at the folded letter Katie still had in her other hand. "Can I read it?"

"Absolutely not."

"Come on." Cassidy tried to snatch the letter from Katie's fingers.

"Quit it." Katie took a step back. "I'm not kidding around. This is private. This is a private correspondence between mother and daughter."

Cassidy took another swipe at the letter. "That only interests me more."

Katie had no choice but to run the letter into her bedroom. She shoved it into her nightstand drawer and then stood in front of it. "Stay back," she said. "And stop being a dick."

"Who are you calling a dick?" Cassidy tugged Katie down

onto her bed, pretended to go in for a kiss, and then dove for the nightstand drawer.

Katie tried to tackle and subdue her, to take Cassidy down with a linebacker blitz, but she was too late, and Cassidy was too quick.

"Whoa. Hold on!" Cassidy pulled something from the drawer, but it wasn't Katie's letter to her mother. "Is this the Boss Lady?"

Katie threw herself onto Cassidy again, this time trying to swipe the hot-pink vibrator out of Cassidy's grasp. "How do you know her name?"

"We've met before." Cassidy allowed herself to finally be taken down by Katie. She pulled her in closer by the waistband of her jeans.

"I am so mad at you right now." Katie pinned Cassidy's wrists to the bed.

"I should be the one who's mad. You've been holding out on me," Cassidy said with a smirk. "We can have some fun with this."

After they had their fun, Katie wrapped her arms around Cassidy's bare torso. "I needed that," she said.

Cassidy kissed her on top of her head. "Me too."

"Work today sucked," Katie said. "And tomorrow's going to suck worse."

Katie was getting accustomed to this—the cuss words that came flying out of her mouth after sex, the rapid-fire jokes and questions, all the ways her postorgasmic euphoria, instead of quieting her, made her giggly and wired.

She was glad she'd been careless enough to leave the bottle of bourbon from her and Cassidy's last bedroom romp in place, because now all she had to do to refill their glasses was reach over to her nightstand. While doing this, she deliberated on whether she should tell Cassidy about her run-in with Gina and Becky at the food festival. Katie was still angry about it. She'd walked away from them feeling offended in a way that was new and unexplainable to her.

People who barely knew Katie made assumptions about her all the time. It came with the territory of being tall and thin with blond hair and blue eyes—not that she was complaining. Though she longed for the day when a man, a coworker, or opposing counsel across a boardroom table didn't automatically assume she wasn't as smart as they were, or that she had gotten where she was because of her looks or some manipulative use of sex.

Maybe Katie was paranoid, maybe they weren't always thinking those things, but she was pretty sure they were.

This, though, was new. Could she honestly be offended by anyone assuming she was straight? Did she really want to read as gay?

"I had a pretty good day," Cassidy said. "In fact, I have a surprise."

"Did you get put on the Credit Suisse deal?" Katie handed Cassidy her glass. "Tell me they chose you over that walking penis you work with, what's his name, Hamlet? Hampus?"

"His name is Hamlin," Cassidy said. "Like in 'The Pied Piper.' And no one's been put on Credit Suisse yet."

"Who was Hamlin in 'The Pied Piper'?"

"Hamelin was the town. He was the Pied Piper of Hamelin."

"Why do you know that?"

"I prosecuted him in mock trial. I argued that he intentionally put the children of Hamelin in harm's way when he lured them from their homes with his magic pipe. Now, do you want to know the surprise or not?"

"I do." Katie sipped her drink. "Please proceed."

"Thank you." Cassidy straightened her posture. "And perhaps you want to brush up on your medieval folklore. I got us tickets to the opera for this weekend. It's a gala, actually. It starts with a cocktail reception, followed by a new production of *Romeo and Juliet*, and then dinner and dancing—What? What's wrong?"

"Nothing." Katie felt her buoyancy sink like a dense chunk of coal.

"You hate the opera."

"No."

"Then why are you making that face?"

"I am making no face." Katie forced an overly chipper smile.

"Is *Romeo and Juliet* not your thing?" Cassidy said. "Too schmaltzy? Were you hoping I was going to say it was a production of *The Pied Piper of Hamelin*?"

"Shit. Okay." Katie gave up on trying to appear less crestfallen. "The opera makes me think of Paul Michael. That's where we went on our first date."

"Oh. Forget it then." Cassidy made a poor attempt to mask her disappointment with nonchalance. "I'll just give the tickets away."

"No," Katie said. "You must have gone to such trouble."

"Not really. I just thought it would be fun to get dressed up and do something fancy, but we can just stay in bed all weekend and order takeout if you want."

Katie thought for a moment. She knew the right answer was not more takeout in bed, and if she was being honest, this onset of opera phobia wasn't just about Paul Michael. It was about her fear of the unknown. What would it be like to go somewhere so proper and public with Cassidy? On a real date out in the real world of regular people. But the look on Cassidy's face told Katie just how much she wanted this. The longer Katie hesitated, the more she could feel the disappointment drumming off Cassidy, and she just couldn't bear it.

"I'm being silly." Katie downed the last of her bourbon. "It'll be fun. We should go. I want to go."

"Are you sure?"

Katie did her best to sound as sure as she knew Cassidy wanted her to be. "Positive," she said. "How fancy is it? Do I wear a gown?"

"It's black tie."

"So what will you wear?" Katie asked.

"A black tie," Cassidy said.

"Right. Okay." Katie reached for the bottle on her nightstand and refilled her drink again.

TWENTY-TWO

··

Cassidy adjusted her bow tie and stepped back to admire her reflection in the mirror. She looked damn good in a tuxedo. Maybe not a purple paisley one like Gerard had threatened to make for her, but this classic two-button with notched lapels did her right.

Of course stepping into the world wearing a tuxedo also brought its own problems. Any event that called for formalwear was, by definition, marked by adherence to strictly proscribed forms. In such a setting a female body in a tuxedo—a tuxedo without a plunging neckline or cropped bottoms paired with stiletto heels, but a proper men's tux—confused the hell out of people. Sometimes it made them angry, as if Cassidy were trying to trick them, like she had some nefarious intention other than just wanting to feel comfortable in her clothes. But as far as Cassidy was concerned it was worth the trouble.

She unbuttoned, then rebuttoned, her jacket, adjusted her shirt collar.

For the most part, people meant no harm, just as she meant no harm, and she never held innocent people's bewilderment against them. Getting called "sir" was no more or less correct than getting called "ma'am" or "miss." None felt exactly right, so it was all the same to Cassidy.

Still, even after all these years of digging in her heels, of refusing to bend to the senseless conventions of the straight world, sometimes it was just plain hard. The last time Cassidy had worn this tux was when her firm bought a charity table at an Audubon Society fund-raiser. It was a stuffy night of lawyer small talk and mingling with bird lovers that culminated in Cassidy's getting stopped in the vestibule of the women's bathroom by a confused attendant. Normally when this happened a simple smile coupled with warm eye contact and a gentle, nonthreatening "It's okay," remedied the situation—but on that night it failed. And of course who came out from one of the stalls in the midst of the escalating spectacle but Cassidy's most senior female partner, drawing all sorts of unnecessary attention, crooning, "What's going on here? This is a woman. I can vouch for her."

Just the memory of it gave Cassidy the sweats, but none of that needed to be on her mind tonight.

Tonight was going to be special, and Cassidy couldn't get

to Lincoln Center fast enough. She flicked a few specks of lint from her jacket sleeve and out the door she went.

Their meeting spot was the fountain in front of the Opera House. Watching it do its watery thing, Cassidy wondered how many other young lovers had set this as their rendezvous point in the past fifty years. How many pennies had been tossed into this falling water and wishes made? There were no coins in Cassidy's formalwear pockets, only paper bills and credit cards bound by a silver money clip—what might the whole stack be worth in wishes if she just plunked it in, clip and all, as an offering?

Cassidy checked her watch, scratched at the back of her head. She was becoming antsy, uncharacteristically anxious and fearful that Katie might not show. Then she spotted Katie coming toward her in a ruffled evening gown with beading that refracted the plaza lights.

Cassidy could barely conceive of her good fortune watching Katie make her way through the crowd, that this was who she was waiting for.

"Hi, handsome," Katie said.

"Hello, beautiful." She kissed Katie on the cheek, then took another look at her. "Your dress . . ."

"Do you like the color? The salesgirl called it—"

"Rose quartz," Cassidy said.

"Yes."

"It's perfect."

They crossed the promenade and entered the theater. Cassidy took a chance and reached for Katie's hand. Katie startled at first, like she might pull away, but didn't.

Just inside, a butler in tails greeted them with a tray of champagne flutes, and Cassidy took one for each of them.

It was almost more than Cassidy's senses could take in, the regal red carpet, the swirling white staircases, chandeliers like diamond fireworks exploding overhead.

In the corner a string quartet played Canon in D, a sadly romantic song that reminded Cassidy of every wedding ceremony she'd ever been to. Katie stopped to watch the musicians from across the floor, their bows moving in perfect harmony across their instruments.

"This is nice," Katie said. "I'm glad we're doing this."

"It's not too weird for you?"

"Not now that we're here reclaiming it as our own."

"I'll drink to that." Cassidy raised her flute and held it there. She found herself striving to verbalize something, to somehow mark this moment. "You know, Katie," she began, "these past few weeks have been— I feel so—"

"You don't even have to say it." Katie sipped her champagne. "I know, it's been crazy."

"But I want to say it." Cassidy forced herself to look Katie directly in the eyes. "This is so not like me, but . . ."

Katie's eyes, Cassidy realized, were fixed somewhere over her shoulder.

"Oh shit," Katie said.

A woman's voice behind Cassidy called out, "Katie, what a surprise. How lovely to see you."

"Lillian, Lincoln, hello." Katie's face curled into a tight smile. "Oh my goodness, you're all here."

Cassidy stepped aside and turned to see a stiff-necked foursome approaching.

Lincoln and Lillian, whose names she recognized from Katie's stories, and just behind them, a string bean of a guy in horn-rimmed glasses who quickly dropped the hand of the panic-stricken blonde at his side. Paul Michael and Amy—it had to be.

This couldn't be happening.

Paul Michael bumped Cassidy's elbow with his when he stepped past her to give Katie a peck on the cheek, and he didn't say *excuse me*.

Cassidy immediately despised him. His severe haircut and weak chin. His boring black suit with black necktie with black shirt that he obviously thought made him look chic but actually made him resemble a nerdy mortician even more than he already did. The man was a straight and narrow line—a flat line in the way of a life expiring on a table.

This was the dude Katie had spent five years with? Who had her heart in his pale, scrawny hand and discarded it? To be with *that* girl? Amy was so routinely pretty, so complacently average. She didn't contain a shard of Katie's magic.

"You look great," Paul Michael said to Katie, while plain-Jane Amy looked down at her plain-Jane shoes. "But this is the last place I ever expected to see you. Who are you here with?"

Cassidy steeled herself. Here it was, the moment of truth. She took a breath and stepped forward, but Katie swiveled away from her.

"I'm here with a date," Katie said. "But he had to step outside to take a call."

Cassidy nearly tripped on her own feet.

"He's a doctor," Katie continued. "So when his phone rings . . ."

"A doctor," Lillian said. "And here we were worried about how you were holding up."

They all laughed, so Katie laughed, but defensively, shamefully.

Cassidy could see it all of a sudden—who Katie was when she was with them. How she strove for their approval. How she submerged her accent and all her spunk, and straightened her posture to match the rigidity of theirs. Even her voice sounded different, cloying in its sweetness, overly eager to please.

"You don't need to worry about me," Katie said to Lillian. "I'm doing great. In fact, I couldn't be better."

Cassidy took a step forward, and another, and another. Her legs were moving on their own, to rescue her by carrying her out of earshot, but she could still hear Katie gushing niceties for Paul Michael's benefit.

Cassidy abandoned her champagne flute on a butler's tray and continued taking steps until she was back outside, where if Katie's pretend doctor date was taking an important call, she may have encountered him. She walked straight past the plaza fountain with all its motherfucking pennies and wishes, to the curb.

She held up her arm to hail a cab.

"Cassidy, wait!" Katie jogged toward her, holding her floor-length gown up to her knees.

Cassidy waved with more vigor for a taxi.

"That was horrible of me, I know." Katie caught her by her nonhailing arm. "I'm sorry."

Cassidy shook her off. "You can't apologize for what you just did."

"I panicked! That was like the worst thing that could have happened. That was every single person I've been avoiding for weeks ambushing me all at once. You have to understand what that was like for me."

"You want me to understand? You made me invisible, Katie. Because you're embarrassed to be seen with me."

"That's not true."

"It is true," Cassidy said. "And I don't need your shame."

"Look, I fucked up, okay?" Katie's voice, back to its normal register, cracked with emotion. "But you can't just leave."

This was where Katie was mistaken. Cassidy could always just leave.

A cab pulled up to the side of the curb, and Cassidy opened the door. "Whatever this was between us, Katie, it just ended."

She got in the cab, slammed the door closed, and told the driver to drive.

TWENTY-THREE

Katie watched Cassidy's cab drive away, then walked in the same direction down Broadway, dirtying her gown's bottom on the filthy sidewalk.

She stopped at Columbus Circle and took a seat on the stone steps beneath the infamous colonizer's statue. All around her couples flirted and kissed and snapped selfies— men, women, young, old, multicultured, multigendered city dwellers and tourists of all stripes. Katie's heartbreak seemed to magnify the way this stone circle could have passed for some jungle watering hole where even the most hunted creatures could gather without fear of being eaten.

If only she and Cassidy had come here to sit, instead of heading into that man-eat-man gala where the vicious predators of Katie's past life lurked and pounced.

Fuck the fucking opera.

She shouldn't have pretended to not be there with Cassidy—Katie knew that. She also shouldn't have been sitting here now. She should have forced herself into Cassidy's taxi, tried harder to apologize, made promises to do better. That's what you do when you really don't want a person to leave you.

But Cassidy was right; Katie had pretended to not be at the opera with Cassidy because she was ashamed to be seen at the opera with Cassidy. The split-second decision to tell the truth or lie to Paul Michael and her former friends was decided automatically, by instinct alone. She lied to sidestep the humiliation of their faces rearranging at the sight of Cassidy in her tuxedo, how their initial confusion would have turned to shock, then slightly more amused shock. Then what?

A skateboarder zipped past Katie, missing her toes by mere inches. He jumped his board up against the stair's edge, then promptly fell on his ass at Katie's feet. Unfazed, he bounced up and chased after his board to try the trick again.

From a rational standpoint Katie understood that she could march back to the opera house right then and set them all straight, and it would be fine.

Paul Michael would use it as validation, say, *That explains so much!* He'd bask in the assumption that their sex was so boring not because he sucked at it, or because their connection was never as strong as they thought, or because they weren't compatible in the least, but because she was a lesbian. How easy that would make it for him, for all of them, to pat themselves on their backs for their betrayal.

Why should she care what they thought of her anyway, when, in truth, she could hardly stand the whole lot of them? She had worked so hard over the years to win them over, convinced her compatibility with Paul Michael was worth the extra effort, but that was just one more way she was mistaken.

Katie thought back to the first time she laid eyes on Paul Michael.

It was only a week into classes at Columbia. A girl from her civil procedure class had invited Katie out with a few other 1Ls to a bar on West End Avenue—and there he was in his Jonathan Franzen glasses and black jacket over black shirt over black jeans, drinking some pretentious cocktail that involved a cherry. If all of New York City were amalgamated into one man, Katie thought at the time, this would be him.

She waited for him to sidle up next to her at the bar, and before even a hello, he reached out to touch the silk scarf she was wearing around her neck. "Hermès?" he asked.

Katie had to keep herself from laughing because she was not in fact a wearer of scarves. This was the first silk scarf her neck had ever seen, which she'd purchased specifically because she thought she might blend in better with the coastal elite if she started accessorizing like them. Hours upon hours had gone into this one silk ornament, choosing just the right pattern, practicing knots in the mirror, deciding the double-wrap French knot was her favorite because it appeared the most nonchalant.

When Paul Michael reached out to rub that scarf between his fingers, this was what he couldn't have known—how the moment had been choreographed by Katie herself. She hadn't fully understood why it mattered so much, at first, to get this one accessory right, but it struck her then. *Aha. Here it is. This is why.*

"Yves Saint Laurent," Katie said, sounding to herself like someone else—and she instantly fell in love with that person.

With that person. Not him. It was so clear to Katie now, how from their very first encounter, it was wrong. She'd never truly loved Paul Michael. She loved that he could get her where she thought she wanted to go.

He was right to leave her.

He was wrong to cheat on her, but they both knew she wouldn't have left him. She would have kept at it, kept trying. Like this skateboarder Katie was watching, who kept eating it on the pavement, over and over again. That Katie wasn't a quitter had always been one of her best qualities, but in this case it meant that she would stay the course in a doomed relationship for better or worse, in sickness and health, in spite of all signs telling her to do the opposite.

How terrifying that her own judgment could be so clouded, that she could so utterly convince herself that whatever discomfort she'd felt, whatever doubts she'd had, were simply her own shortcomings to overcome. She'd actually thought she was being brave by insisting upon him in spite of not only her family's disapproval but also that quiet voice from deep down inside her own guts.

Katie rubbed her bare arms to warm them against the cold. What were her guts whispering to her now? That she should go home?

That she should go to Cassidy's.

No, she should go home.

"Are you a princess?"

Katie turned to find a little girl wearing a pink tiara looking up at her.

"No," Katie said.

The girl's face dropped, and Katie realized her error. "Are *you* a princess?" she quickly asked.

"Yes!" The girl laughed and ran back to her mother.

Katie perused her surroundings, realizing how strange she must look sitting alone in her rose quartz gown among these tourists and lovers and skateboarders.

She stood up to go, waved goodbye to her tiara'd friend,

and lifted the hem of her dress as she made her way to the street.

⤜♡⤛

Right about now Romeo and Juliet were probably somewhere in the Capulets' orchard wishing that morning was not upon them. Katie and Cassidy might have been holding hands in the dark, flushed and fevered, their own chemistry amplified by the passion of the performers onstage.

Instead Katie was seated alone at her kitchen table, subduing her heightened emotions with a task. She stared at the pen in her hand; her customary salutation, *Dear Mama*; and the following blank page.

What you're about to read, Katie began, *is a feeble attempt to puncture my inflated sadness by bringing pen to paper and accomplishing something productive. The contents of this letter will in no way reflect my current state of mind or the fact that my life is in pieces.*

Okay. She'd gotten that out of her system. Now she could begin again with a fresh sheet of paper.

Dear Mama, I'm writing to you after a long, exciting evening.

Katie gazed around her neglected kitchen, at the smattering of spilled coffee grounds on the countertop, the slowly dripping faucet.

It's actually been an exciting few weeks.

She looked around some more, this time at the faded photos stuck with magnets to her refrigerator door. The one of her as a little girl riding her favorite horse struck her, at the moment, like a punch in the stomach. Was there anything left in the world that wouldn't somehow make her think of Cassidy?

Katie rose from her chair to yank the photo down but got distracted by the one next to it—her at fifteen with her parents and brothers, all of them posed in color-coordinated outfits. Why would she want to have this outdated version of her family staring back at her every time she opened the refrigerator? It'd been up there so long, she'd stopped seeing it.

But Katie really looked at the photo now, and she remembered that day. She and her mother had gone to get their hair and nails done in the morning, and then the whole family had piled into the car and headed for Sears. It had been a sunny, warm afternoon in April, but just as they stepped out of the car, a full parking lot's length from the store's entrance, the heavens opened and it started to pour. Her mother screamed bloody murder, like it was a vat of pig's blood that'd been dumped on her head, and the four of them ran through sheets of rain laughing so hard, because there was just nothing to be done.

You couldn't even tell any of that had happened by the

picture. The line at the Sears portrait studio was long enough that they'd all dried off, and Sue Ellen at the hair salon had used enough hairspray on her mother that no amount of rain was bringing down anyone's updo. The photo turned out perfect.

Tears started falling from Katie's eyes then. She returned the photo to its place on the refrigerator door and looked to her letter.

She took her pen in hand and sat.

There's something important I need to tell you, Katie wrote. *So I'm going to stop beating around the bush.*

Nope.

Katie crossed out that last line, taking extra care to fully blacken out the word *bush.*

The truth, she wrote, *is that I've met someone and I believe I'm in love.*

But it's a woman I've fallen in love with, Mama. And I don't know what that means, or if it means anything different about me, but I don't want to lie to you about who I've been spending my time with.

More tears rolled down Katie's cheeks as she imagined what it would be like for her tough and sometimes difficult and often fearful mother to read these words. Her mother who had always done the best she could to love Katie the best she could.

Her name is Cassidy. She's a born-and-bred New Yorker

and who knows if you will like her very much, but I do. I truly do.

I want to continue spending time with her, so that I can get to know her better, and it would be great if I could share that process with you, but I understand how this is asking a lot.

I need you now more than ever, Mama. And I love you more than ever, too. I hope that once the understandable shock of this has worn off, you'll see that I'm still the same Katie you've always loved so much.

When she was finished writing, Katie set down her pen and folded the letter into thirds. She reached for an envelope from her stationery box—and then paused.

There was something she needed to do first, before sending this off. She quickly got dressed and slipped the letter into the inside pocket of her jacket.

꒰♡꒱

It was Brandon, not Frank, on duty in the lobby of Cassidy's building. Katie greeted him as she headed straight for the elevator. "Is Cassidy in?"

"I don't think so," he said. "But I'll check."

"Oh." Katie's forward momentum came to a halt. She hadn't considered that Cassidy might not be home when she sped out of her apartment and across town on this mission.

Brandon called up to Cassidy's room. "No answer."

"Oh," Katie said again. She couldn't have come all this

way for nothing. "Well, she said she'd be here in just a few minutes."

Brandon hung up the phone and eyeballed Katie like he sensed something was suspicious.

"Can you let me up?" Katie asked. "She gave me a key, but I misplaced it. We'll have a new one made tomorrow."

Brandon hesitated, then nodded and smiled. "Of course." He fetched Cassidy's spare key from wherever it lived and politely led Katie up to Cassidy's floor.

It was true; Cassidy wasn't home. The apartment was pitch black when Brandon opened the door.

He clicked on the lights. "Can I help you with anything else?"

"No," Katie said. "You've been very helpful, thank you."

Brandon exited, and Katie shut and locked the door behind him.

Should she text Cassidy to tell her she was there?

If she did, Cassidy might flip out. She had been so angry when she left Katie at the opera—and she had every right to be.

No. Katie would just sit on the couch and wait.

She took the letter from her jacket pocket, unfolded it, and read it over.

When Cassidy arrived home, Katie would apologize and then she would show her this. She would explain how she understood that it was the twenty-first century, but that her family was stuck somewhere in the late 1950s—and that parts of herself were, too.

I'm sorry for my failings, she would say. *But my feelings are real.* She would tell Cassidy that she wanted to try. She would beg for another chance.

Just then Katie heard footsteps coming from the hallway beyond the door—then voices.

It was definitely Cassidy. And someone else?

A female someone else.

Oh no.

Katie heard the jangling of keys and ran for Cassidy's bedroom.

They entered the apartment, and their voices were muffled for a moment. No one seemed to notice that the lights had been left on.

Then Cassidy said, "Can I fix you a drink?"

"Thank you," the woman said, in what Katie believed was a European accent. "If you bring to me in the bedroom."

The bedroom? Fuck fuck.

Katie dashed for the closet and silently closed the door.

The ironic absurdity of this hiding spot was not lost on Katie, but the fact of the matter was there was no better place to take cover when you'd sort of accidentally broken into someone's apartment.

In the dark, surrounded by all of Cassidy's clothes—her

suits and sport coats and custom dress shirts, her leather boots and oxfords—Katie covered her mouth and prayed.

Oh god. Please don't open the closet door.

Cassidy had followed the woman into the bedroom, laughing. They sounded a little drunk.

Katie stood very still, surveilling the slip of light coming from the crack beneath the closet door.

Cassidy and the woman were quiet for a few seconds.

Then Katie heard what she was fairly certain was dirty talk in Italian.

The bed squeaked.

Cassidy let out a barely perceptible grunt. Katie knew that grunt. She'd grown to love that grunt.

She couldn't take this. She couldn't be here for this.

Katie was poised to throw open the closet door, to yell, *Stop! Please stop!*

TWENTY-FOUR

Cassidy sipped her scotch alone at the bar, her bow tie an unraveled black ribbon at her elbow.

"Buy me a drink?" Gina climbed onto the vacant stool beside her.

Cassidy raised a finger toward Dahlia, who immediately set down a rocks glass for Gina and poured her a double.

"Can I have a Budweiser?" Gina said.

Dahlia grimaced, poured the contents of Gina's glass into Cassidy's.

"I tried to tell her," she said to Gina while popping the cap off a bottle of Bud. "Look on the bright side; at least this happened while we're still here. But she's not having much looking on the bright side."

"Want to talk about it?" Gina twirled Cassidy's discarded bow tie around her fingers.

"Nope," Cassidy said.

"I'll go mess that bitch up right now, C, I'm not even kidding."

"I brought it on myself. You tried to warn me."

"That's true. But I'm sorry I was right."

Cassidy shook her head. "I must be getting soft in my old age."

"Nah." Gina yanked off her knit beanie and scratched at her fauxhawk. "You just need to get with someone tonight, get back to feeling like yourself."

"Not this time."

"Well you can't just sit here looking like a groom who got stood up at the altar. You're embarrassing yourself." Gina tugged her beanie back on. "I heard Becky's got a cousin in town from Italy who looks like a young Sophia Loren. They're on their way here. You should tap that."

Cassidy crumpled her discarded bow tie into a ball and shoved it into her tuxedo jacket pocket. "Do you even know who Sophia Loren is?"

"No, but she sounds hot. And the point is, who better to fuck the pain away than a visiting Italian cousin?"

"I know you're only trying to help," Cassidy said. "But please stop trying to help."

"Can I give you some real talk?" Gina swiveled around on her stool and squared her shoulders to Cassidy. "We both know this thing with Katie was never going to work. It's better she screwed you over. If she didn't, you would've gotten her to the point where she was totally devoted to you and then freaked out on her and bounced. Or, more likely, you would've freaked out and cheated on her so she'd leave you. So stop this feeling sorry for yourself. All that's happened is she beat you to the punch."

Cassidy swallowed some scotch to wash down the emotion creeping up her throat.

"You should write her a goddamn thank-you note," Gina said. "For saving you the time. Also, look."

Cassidy turned to follow Gina's gaze to where Becky was escorting her cousin into the bar.

The girl did have something old-world movie star about her.

"She's beautiful," Gina said. "And I bet you could get her to make out with you, at the very least."

Cassidy didn't care if she could or couldn't. Whether the girl made out with her or not didn't matter nearly as much as the trying.

"She's coming over." Gina hopped off her barstool to free it up for the Italian.

"Cassidy, *come va?*" Becky escorted her cousin, who bore no family resemblance whatsoever to the chef, to the bar like a trophy wife. "I want you to meet Emiliana. Doesn't she look like a young Sophia Loren?"

"I wish you would stop saying that," Emiliana said.

"Nice to meet you." Cassidy took the girl's hand in hers but resisted going in for a European-style double cheek kiss like an American idiot.

"Cassidy's a cater waiter," Becky said. "That's why she's wearing the monkey suit."

"She's kidding," Cassidy said. "I'm an attorney."

Emiliana touched the fabric of Cassidy's lapel, then examined the stitching just inside her jacket's hem. "Good quality," she said. "No waiter suit." Her thick accent was definitely appealing.

"I was at the opera earlier," Cassidy said.

"Oh?"

"Cassidy's what you might call a Casanova," Becky interjected. "*Il stronzino. Capisce?*"

"*Sì?*" Emiliana gave a nod to Becky but kept her eyes on Cassidy. "She said you're a little asshole."

"She's lying," Cassidy said. "I'm a big asshole."

Emiliana laughed.

♡

Cassidy and Emiliana made their way into Cassidy's apartment, overcoming their tepid language barrier with raw physicality.

Cassidy was no longer a person; she was a vehicle in motion, fueled by self-loathing and a willful disregard for her own misgivings.

"Can I fix you a drink?" she asked, stupefied by her own relentless soberness. Emiliana was a blurred vision—a cinched waist in a black dress, bare legs to the thigh—but Cassidy could still see her clearly enough to remember she wasn't Katie.

Emiliana kicked off her shoes and drifted toward the bedroom, and Cassidy wondered, Who is this person and why is she here? But she still followed after her.

No, Cassidy was not drunk enough for this, and yet they were on her bed, and the girl was whispering incomprehensible Italian into her ear.

Cassidy untied the strap holding her shirtdress closed, and Emiliana wiggled it completely off. Her olive skin was suntanned and smoothed by warm coastal sands. She could have been an advertisement for the Italian Riviera or the island of Capri. But Cassidy's own body went cold.

"Fuck," she said.

"Yes," Emiliana said. "This is why I came."

"I know. I'm sorry." Cassidy climbed off her. "But this is a mistake. I can't do this." Cassidy swiveled around to standing. "You've got to go."

"*Sei serio?*"

"Yes, serious," Cassidy said. "I'm in love with someone else."

Emiliana made no move to put her dress back on, from

either pure disbelief or confusion as to why loving someone else should matter.

Cassidy gestured at the doorway. "You have to leave."

"*Vaffanculo*," Emiliana said. She reached for her dress, finally.

"Whatever that means, I'm sure you're right." Cassidy searched her pants pockets for some cash and stuffed a few bills into Emiliana's hand. "Here's cab fare."

Cassidy escorted her out of her apartment, to the hallway, into the elevator. She watched as Emiliana gave her the universal sign of the middle finger as the elevator doors closed on her like a curtain.

Only when Emiliana was safely on her way down to the lobby could Cassidy breathe again.

Why the hell did she have to bring someone home? She double-locked her apartment door and marched back into the bedroom, then stood there for a moment, unsure of what to do next.

All her life Cassidy could give up on anyone. A switch got flipped and that was it. No looking back. Katie had hurt her deeply, and yet she still didn't want to never talk to her again. Instead she wanted to forgive her. The difference wasn't something Cassidy could put into words but something she could feel in her soul. She couldn't let Katie go.

Cassidy hunted the bedroom for her tuxedo jacket. She

found it on the floor at the foot of her bed and felt around for her phone.

They should have talked more. Katie might not have melted down at the opera if they'd simply addressed the fact that she hadn't had the years of practice Cassidy did growing accustomed to being different, to looking different. Learning to disregard random disapproval and being stared at, and liking yourself anyway. And perhaps the most difficult at first—telling the world you've changed.

Cassidy found her phone, scrolled to Katie's name. She sat on the edge of her bed and pressed *call*.

Katie couldn't promise her anything—Cassidy understood that, and she couldn't promise Katie anything either—but she still wanted to try. Even if it meant they would have to go slow, and do hard work, and overcome challenges, and talk about emotions, and do all that corny lesbian shit that Cassidy couldn't stand.

She waited for Katie's phone to ring.

TWENTY-FIVE

Katie stopped herself just in time from hurling open Cassidy's closet door.

"This is a mistake," she heard. "I can't do this. You've got to go."

Cassidy was damn right the girl had to go. What was she doing here in the first place? Could Cassidy not even take twenty-four hours to process what had happened between them? What the hell was up with that?

"I'm in love with someone else," Cassidy said.

Katie heard it clear as day, as if she were right there in bed with them and not hiding among Cassidy's neckties.

Love was definitely the word Cassidy had used, and it made Katie feel a little less silly about the letter in her jacket pocket, the letter she'd run here with certain it would make a difference if only Cassidy would read it.

There were a few minutes of silence now as Katie tried to figure out what was happening, but she was pretty sure the European was getting kicked to the curb. Then the apartment door slammed shut, followed by footsteps back in the bedroom.

Cassidy was alone now and moving around, but what was she doing? Had Katie just blown her only chance to safely creep out of her hiding spot?

A few more minutes passed, and Katie began to sweat. How long would she actually have to stay in here? It was only a matter of time before she would need to pee, and Cassidy worshipped her shoes way too much for Katie to defile one by using it as a makeshift Porta Potty. And could a shoe even contain a liquid without leaking all over the place? What about a boot? A galosh might do the trick.

Just then Katie's cell phone vibrated in her pocket.

Shit. Shit. She was scrambling to silence it when she saw Cassidy's name was lit up on its screen. It illuminated the entire dark closet.

Katie looked from the phone to the door to the phone, and it vibrated again.

Why did she click *answer*? She could have just as easily sent the call to voicemail and waited to see if Cassidy would leave a message, but it was too late now. Katie brought the phone to her ear.

"Hello," Cassidy said. "Katie?"

Katie swallowed hard.

"Are you there?" Cassidy's voice came through in stereo.

"I'm here," Katie said into her phone, just as she opened the closet door.

"Jesus Christ!" Cassidy flew off her bed, dropping her phone to the floor. "You scared the shit out of me!" She was still wearing half a tuxedo, black pants and white dress shirt untucked, its top two buttons undone.

"I'm sorry." Katie ended the call and returned her phone to her jacket pocket.

"What the hell are you doing here?" Cassidy was clutching her chest.

"I came to talk to you," Katie said. "I thought you'd be home, but then . . ."

"This is so not okay." Cassidy glanced at her bed as if to make sure the European was in fact gone, and then back at Katie. "You are literally breaking and entering right now."

"I heard you." Katie stepped forward. "I heard that you love me."

"You only heard that because you were spying on me."

"The breaking-and-entering thing is a technicality. There wasn't really any breaking. And I was only spying on you because you brought home a stranger to try to forget me."

Cassidy seemed to harden at the accusation. "Just so we're clear, I haven't done anything wrong. You're the one who fucked up. Not me."

"You're right," Katie said. "I know that. I was just . . ." She paused. "But didn't you just call me? Why did you do that?"

"I have no idea." Cassidy stared down at the floor. "Moment of weakness, I guess."

"You have every right to not forgive me if that's what you choose," Katie said. "But what happened at the opera was a mistake I won't make twice." She waited for Cassidy to say something, but she didn't. "I want to be in this with you," Katie continued. "I really do. Because I love you, too. That's what I came here to tell you."

Some of the fight came out of Cassidy's posture then, and Katie seized the opportunity to take a cautious step closer to her. "But I also have to start being honest about how I'm not as comfortable with myself as you are. And I'm definitely not excited about bringing you home to meet my family, and I don't think they like gay people, and I never wanted to be gay, and I don't even know if I am, but I do like having sex with you and I like *you*. I like everything about you. I'm in love with you even though it's totally complicated."

"That's kind of a lot," Cassidy said, but she didn't back away.

"I want us to be together," Katie said. "And I want everyone to know it."

"Everyone?" Cassidy eyed Katie with lawyerly suspicion.

"Everyone. If you give me the chance, I'll prove it to you." Katie put out her hand.

Cassidy just stared at it.

"Do we have a deal?" Katie asked.

Cassidy was quiet for a minute, and Katie held her breath. The only sound came from the hallway outside, one of Cassidy's neighbors cackling past her door. For a split second Katie feared it was the European back for more.

Then Cassidy took Katie's hand in hers and gave it a firm shake. "I think I might be able to agree to that," she said, and pulled Katie closer.

The sudden nearness of Cassidy's body to hers, its heat— Katie had never been so sure of wanting anything in her life.

She guided Cassidy by the hand toward the bed. "Great," she said. "Moving on then." She lay down, pulling Cassidy on top of her. "Want to get out of these clothes?"

"Yes," Cassidy said.

TWENTY-SIX

Cassidy didn't want to go to Metropolis's last night. Sentimentality gave her the sweats and she preferred digesting her sadness quietly and alone, but Katie told her to stop being a pussy and to let herself feel some feelings, so that was that.

As expected, the night was bathed in an in-memoriam-like nostalgia, but Dahlia mercifully drew the line at the music she allowed from the overhead speakers. No "Candle in the Wind." No "Tears in Heaven." No "Hallelujah." Absolutely no Sarah McLachlan. Just the regular mix of never-too-earnest pop rock that usually soundtracked their nights at the Met, but at a slightly lower volume than normal.

Everyone sat in their regular places in the corner near the pool table, with the addition of Katie at Cassidy's side, and the group relished having her fresh ears to listen to their favorite memories.

Gina rolled a pool cue in her hands. "Remember the time I accidentally started that fire and no one noticed till like the whole bar was filled with smoke?"

"Yeah," Becky said. "I'm the one who put it out with my beer, and I never got a free refill."

"Here." Dahlia handed over her pint glass of vodka soda. "For your heroism."

"Better late than never." Becky tossed Dahlia's straw onto the floor and took a sip.

Gina stood up to take a shot at the pool game she was playing against herself. "What about the night that girl peed in the mop closet?"

"That girl was crazy," Cassidy said. "But that was hilarious."

"Not hilarious." Dahlia, having given up her pint glass to Becky, sipped directly from the bottle of vodka she'd brought over from behind the bar. "We couldn't even clean it up because it was all on the mops. And there was a bucket right there. She could have just as easily done her business into the bucket instead of all over the floor."

"It was hilarious," Cassidy said into Katie's ear.

"What about whipped-cream wrestling nights?" Becky said.

Cassidy grabbed hold of Dahlia's vodka bottle and took a

swig. "I remember how that shit smelled on everyone's skin when it started to sour."

"Yeah, the dairy element hadn't really been thought through," Becky said. "Baby-oil wrestling nights were way better."

"But slipperier," Cassidy said. "Who was that girl who slid across the floor and fell on her ass?"

"Who knows?" Dahlia reclaimed the vodka. "We never saw her again after that night."

"Strip Twister, though," Gina said.

Strip Twister was the bomb, everyone agreed.

Katie was amused, or at least it seemed that way to Cassidy in her increasingly inebriated state.

At some point, Katie took Cassidy's chin into her hand, turned her face left, then right.

"You're wasted," she said.

Cassidy closed one eye. "A bit, I think yes."

"A rare opportunity to take advantage of you." Katie stood. "Come with me."

Cassidy followed. "Where are we going?"

Katie led her across the bar, to the bathroom, where Cassidy tried to decipher if she might actually be too drunk to have sex.

Inside the stall that hadn't had a door since the night some girls swung on it till it fell off its hinges, Katie brought her lips to Cassidy's and kissed her softly. The whole time,

Cassidy was thinking, *This'll be the last time I ever kiss a girl in here.* It was a strange and bittersweet realization to have while this woman she loved, the first she was willing to call girlfriend, had her tongue in her mouth.

Katie pulled away then, and reached into her jeans pocket.

Cassidy looked to see what she had in her hand: two markers.

Katie pulled the cap off one of them. "Would you believe this is the first time I've ever done this?" She located an un-claimed section of mottled tile and in hot-pink ink wrote the words *Katie loves Cassidy.* Then she used the other marker to lasso this declaration in a bold red heart.

Cassidy touched it with her hand, the ink already set. She imagined how this very tile would be demolished, immortal-ized from sordid ceramic to sacred dust. Which would have been the case if later in the night—it wasn't clear to Cassidy exactly when—the looting hadn't happened.

It must have been nearing four a.m. when the night really went into overdrive. Nobody was sober, and nothing was off limits as a keepsake. People pocketed shot glasses and claimed favorite pool cues. They raided various tchotchkes on display behind the bar—a pair of rainbow handcuffs; an autographed DVD of season four of *The L Word*; a figurine of Scar, the evil gay lion from *The Lion King.* Becky took custody of the tattered magazine cover of Ellen DeGeneres declaring, "Yep, I'm Gay," that had probably been taped to that spot on the wall since 1997.

This part Cassidy was certain of—it was Dahlia herself who retrieved her security hammer from its shelf beneath the cash register. The one they all called MC Hammer, that normally made an appearance only when someone, usually a drunk dude or two, got overly aggressive and needed to be asked to leave. Over the years, the hammer itself had become a verb. As in, "Hey, Dahlia, I think those guys over there need to be MC Hammered out of here."

What prompted Dahlia to raise the mighty MC high in the air with enough fury that more than one person ducked? Who knew?

She handed it off to Gina. "Go, little one," she said. "I beseech you . . . Leave no tile in place!"

Gina lunged for the thing, swung it around with a two-handed grip like it was the sword from *Braveheart*. A throng of drunken madwomen abetted her with war cries, while marching en masse toward the bathroom.

The sound of the first smash was thrilling. It was followed by cheers, and more smashing.

The Best Fucks List fell from the wall in fragments. A scrum of girls scuffled for its scraps as if they were candy from a piñata. Years' worth of arguments, debates, rivalries, love lost, and worries forgotten—the tangible proof they had been there, they existed, they mattered—all of it got MC Hammered.

Everyone left with a piece. A broken, irregular part of something that forevermore would remain incomplete.

That was the moment that it finally sunk in for Cassidy—that the Met, her Met, her wild youth, was truly over. She forced herself to see it, the image of the place shuttered, metal gates rolled down, green plywood affixed to its façade, its ending. And she bid it a fond and gracious goodbye.

Cassidy managed to save the tile encompassing Katie's heart. The way Gina took the hammer to it, it had split in two, but Cassidy was able to retrieve both halves.

It hung on Cassidy's bathroom wall at home now, both sides joined, a crooked line down its middle, with jagged, sharp edges.

EPILOGUE

Katie and Cassidy were walking along Macdougal Street with their hands dug deep into their winter coats when they halted at the sight of a new empty storefront.

"I don't believe it," Cassidy said.

Katie eyed the vacated space, all plywood and papered-over windows. "What closed now?"

"The luxury soap store." Cassidy cracked a smile. "Remember? The one Gina licked a soap cupcake in that time."

"The one that used to be the wine bar." Katie's face lit up with recognition. "And now it's . . ." She trailed off.

"This is where we met," Cassidy said. "Kind of. Right in this spot is where we bumped into each other by accident that first night."

"You're so cute when you get romantic." Katie pulled

Cassidy toward the For Rent sign in the window. "You know what this space would be perfect for?"

"Not overpriced soap, that's for sure."

"Seriously?" Katie gestured at the vacant storefront, which occupied the ground floor of a late-nineteenth-century triplex. "Are you not thinking what I'm thinking?"

Cassidy was quiet for a few seconds. "You think I should—"

"We should," Katie said.

Cassidy raised an eyebrow. "Most lesbians opt for a U-Haul after a few weeks of dating. This would be different."

"Since when do you do anything the way other people do it?" Katie said.

Cassidy looked up and down the street, a strip half transformed by acai bowls and avocado toast, the other half choking to hold on to the artistic grit of a bygone era. "It would be a terrible financial decision."

Katie wrapped her arm around Cassidy's elbow. "I've been meaning to hawk my engagement ring and do something special with the money. Plus I've got this dumb painting that sort of looks like the face of a melting Keith Richards that Paul Michael gave me for our one-year anniversary—because that was just what I wanted. Anyway, it's turned out to be worth a small fortune."

Cassidy let that sink in for a minute. "Dahlia's been looking for a place to run. And Becky would probably throw in with us. She'd make us sell pork sandwiches or something, but I suppose there are worse things than a little pulled pork to keep a crowd happy."

"Spoken like a true Southerner." Katie drew Cassidy in closer.

Arm in arm, they let the air of possibility settle over them, each of them picturing their future shared history.

"It's bound to do better than luxury soap," Cassidy said. "Right?"

"We'll make sure it's the opposite of luxury soap. This'll be way more fun." Katie smiled. "And dirty."

Acknowledgments

I would like to thank my agent, Kerry Sparks, for her early support of the concept of this book, for urging me forward when I needed courage, and always offering a steady hand when I required saving from an anxiety-fueled spinout.

Thank you to Kerri Kolen, whose discerning, perceptive edits helped me bring to life the story she understood I had in my heart.

Thank you to Helen Richard, Sally Kim, Ivan Held, and Christine Ball for their continued support and encouragement in ushering this book into the world, and to the entire crackerjack Putnam team, especially Katie Grinch, Elena Hershey, Alexis Welby, Ashley McClay, Brennin Cummings, Carolyn Darr, and Anabel Pasarow.

To Helen Pennock, I can never thank you enough for all the

ways you helped make this novel possible, from our Saturday-morning brainstorms to your willingness to read and reread drafts, and for believing me every time I said to spare my feelings and tell me what wasn't working, and then enduring me while I sulked over whatever you suggested wasn't working. Sometimes I can hardly believe my great fortune in getting to share my life with you. I love you so much.

To all the queer spaces that embraced me in my greener days . . . Honorable mentions to: Meow Mix, the Hole, Metropolitan, Cattyshack, and Ginger's.

And finally, to everyone I partied with throughout my twenties. You know who you are. Thanks for the memories.

WHEN
Katie
MET
Cassidy

CAMILLE PERRI

A Conversation with Camille Perri

Discussion Guide

BOOK
ENDS

PUTNAM
— EST. 1838 —

A Conversation with Camille Perri

What is your book, _When Katie Met Cassidy_, about?

When Katie Met Cassidy is a romantic comedy about gender and sexuality. Katie Daniels, a perfection-seeking twenty-eight-year-old heretofore straight woman with a strong set of traditional values, encounters and is drawn to Cassidy Price, a gay, promiscuous, gender-nonconforming lawyer. Katie and Cassidy start to fall in love, and as a result, each begins to look at herself through new eyes and reevaluate her trajectory.

At its core, the novel is about the importance of figuring out who we are, in order to go after what we truly want.

Tell us a little bit about the main characters, Katie and Cassidy.

Katie was born and raised in Kentucky. She's a good girl, a people pleaser, and a rule follower. Cassidy is a native New Yorker—who, at first glance, Katie mistakes for a man. Katie likes to wear dresses. Cassidy likes to wear custom-made men's suits.

A close reader will notice they're both highly concerned with appearances, but it displays itself in opposite ways. Katie's driving characteristic is that she wants approval. It's hard for her not to be liked and this affects many of her decisions. Cassidy's driving characteristic is that way deep down she yearns to be loved, but she behaves in ways completely antithetical to that. Simply put: Cassidy needs to be loved, while Katie needs to be liked. This is the root of much of their conflict.

The book is a twist on the traditional "boy meets girl." Why did you feel it was important to showcase Katie and Cassidy's relationship using the format of a romantic comedy?

In gender and sexuality studies, there's a concept called "queering," which basically means reevaluating or culturally reappropriating something with an eye toward sexuality and gender. With *When Katie Met Cassidy*, I'm queering the traditional romantic comedy. What I consider radical about this book is that no one dies or gets sick, no one suffers a tragic identity-based misfortune—which is unfortunately often the case when it comes to stories that involve the LGBTQ community.

In general, I'm also a fan of simple stories with complicated emotions.

When Katie meets Cassidy's tight-knit group of friends at the bar Metropolis, she glimpses a world she's never seen before. What aspects of lesbian culture were most important to you to portray?

Aside from the pure wild abandon that happens when there are no straight men around, it was important to me to illustrate just how much the queer community really is a *community*, and how queer spaces are essential to that. I wanted to show how this Metropolis group, many of whom may have been outcasts in the places they're from, or grew up misunderstood, are finally, in the confines of this dilapidated bar, free to be themselves in whatever shape or form that takes.

Katie, as someone who grew up in a strong family-oriented setting, is struck by this—the extent to which these characters she's introduced to through Metropolis serve as one another's families. This is certainly true for Cassidy, who we understand grew up with lukewarm support from her parents.

Popular culture has begun to embrace women taking charge of their sexuality—with TV shows such as *Broad City* and *Girls* reaching large audiences. Do you think mainstream audiences are ready for a book that celebrates women rejecting traditional roles, as Katie and Cassidy do?

As someone who's been thinking critically about these issues since the late 90s, and who's known since then that I would one day try to write a novel tackling this subject, it is almost unbelievable to me just how much mainstream audiences are not only ready for a book that celebrates women rejecting traditional roles, but are starving for it.

There's a lot of sex in this book. Are there challenges to writing a good sex scene?

Is there a lot of sex in this book? I hadn't noticed.

Yes, rule of thumb when it comes to writing a good sex scene is Just Don't. Conventional writer's wisdom says the same thing about attempting humor—tread carefully! I guess I like to live on the edge.

Many books about self-acceptance and sexuality feature characters just at the cusp of adulthood, but Katie, at twenty-eight, and Cassidy, at age thirty, are adults with successful careers. Why did you choose to write a book with characters at this stage in their lives?

I chose these ages for Katie and Cassidy for very specific reasons. I wanted them to already be a bit deep into the groove of their lives, to make it that much harder on them when everything gets shaken up. I'm also fascinated by what happens to many of us around twenty-seven, twenty-eight (what astrologists and many lesbians would refer to as the Saturn Return). You're already an adult, but that very idea— whoa, when did I become an adult?—can be a jolt.

At twenty-eight, Katie is looking at her life and all of a sudden thinking: How is it possible that I'm this age and I'm still not totally sure who I am? Cassidy, at thirty, has passed through this already, but is still clinging to her youth with everything she's got. Cassidy's deal is that she recognizes she's aging out of her lifestyle but isn't sure what kind of life she wants to age into.

I'd also like to add that many, many people "come out" or unexpectedly change their line of thinking in regard to desire and sexuality much later in life than the cusp of adulthood. I wanted to write about this kind of change, which obviously gets much less treatment.

When Katie Met Cassidy is a light-hearted book, but it addresses real issues of LGBTQ identity. What do you hope readers will take away from it?

I definitely set out to write this book in a way that would appeal equally to "straight" and "queer" readers. This is the main reason I chose to alternate between Katie's and Cassidy's points of view. Depending on what personal experience you bring to this novel, Katie might be your touchstone or Cassidy might be your touchstone. For some readers a story about a successful, desirable, unapologetic queer woman is what will resonate most deeply. For others, what will be most interesting is the story of a woman not in the queer community, and not at all wired that way, finding herself attracted to a woman for the first time. Either way, everyone gets to experience all of it. And first and foremost my top priority was to write a fun, highly accessible, and entertaining story.

It's been a tumultuous few years in politics. Does this book's message that "love is love" stand out as radical in the current social and political climate?

I was about three-quarters of the way done with this book when the electoral college epic fail of the election of Donald Trump happened. Suddenly writing a novel felt existentially pointless. But after a few weeks of mourning, I realized how important it was to remember the ways the personal is political and the political is personal. Visibility, representation, and protecting our freedom to be who we want to be, and love who we want to love, felt more imperative than ever.

When Katie Met Cassidy isn't about politics, but the fact that it exists is political. A celebratory queer love story in the midst of all the hatred and bigotry present in our daily collective conscious is, as far as I'm concerned, a form of resistance.

You are active in the queer community. Have you brought any of your own past experiences to the novel?

I honestly feel like I've been collecting material for this novel my entire life. That said, none of the events in the book happened to me, and neither Katie nor Cassidy is intended to be a stand-in for me in any way. The emotional heart of the book though, that's real. And the part about girls wrestling one another on filthy barroom floors. That's also real.

Will we see more of Katie and Cassidy in a forthcoming book?

I don't have any plans to write a sequel to this book, but I do feel like Katie and Cassidy's story, and the stories of all the characters we encounter at the Met, have the potential to evolve. We'll see what form that takes. For now I'm keeping an open mind.